bad power

Deborah Biancotti

First published in Australia in October 2011
by Twelfth Planet Press

www.twelfthplanetpress.com

All works © 2011 Deborah Biancotti

Design and layout by Amanda Rainey
Typeset in Sabon MT Pro

National Library of Australia Cataloguing-in-Publication entry

Author: Biancotti, Deborah.

Title: Bad power : a Twelve Planets collection / by Deborah
                Biancotti, edited by Alisa Krasnostein.

ISBN: 9780980827484 (pbk.)

Other Authors/Contributors:
                Krasnostein, Alisa.

Dewey Number: A823.4

For my family. All of you.

Also From
Twelfth Planet Press

TWELVE PLANETS:

Nightsiders, by Sue Isle

Love and Romanpunk, by Tansy Rayner Roberts

Thief of Lives, by Lucy Sussex

ANTHOLOGIES / COLLECTIONS:

2012, edited by Alisa Krasnostein and Ben Payne

New Ceres Nights, edited by Alisa Krasnostein
and Tehani Wessely

A Book of Endings, by Deborah Biancotti

Glitter Rose, by Marianne de Pierres

Sprawl, edited by Alisa Krasnostein

NOVELLA SERIES:

Angel Rising, by Dirk Flinthart

Horn, by Peter M. Ball

Siren Beat, by Tansy Rayner Roberts /
Roadkill, by Robert Shearman

Bleed, by Peter M. Ball

The Company Articles of Edward Teach, by Thoraiya Dyer /
The Angælien Apocalypse, by Matthew Crulew

Above, by Stephanie Campisi /
Below, by Ben Peek

Table of Contents

Introduction

I first met Deborah Biancotti on a trip to Australia several years ago. I fell in love with the country and have maintained close contact with many of the talented writers I met there. I am pleased and honoured to be writing this introduction to Biancotti's Twelve Planets collection *Bad Power*.

In just five short stories Biancotti manages to create a new world that is strange and yet oh-so-familiar—her characters interact with each other across all these tales as they try to deal with the powers they've acquired and all I can say is I want to read more.

These appetisingly wicked stories give you the perfect taste of Biancotti's talents. "Shades of Grey" shows how the wrong power can be a bad thing as the wealthy Grey continues to seek ways to test his limits and punish himself for his ability to self-heal and possible immortality. We also meet the unusually gifted Detective Palmer—she seems to get all the *interesting* cases.

In "Palming the Lady" a young medical student is stalked by an older homeless woman and continually berated by his famous doctor father. Detective Palmer takes up this case, too, and can't seem to figure out what the homeless woman means about the 'bigger picture'. Not until later, anyway.

"Web of Lies" continues the story of Matthew Webb, that tortured medical student, and how he deals with his father's death and his own growing powers. In "Bad Power" Biancotti introduces us to a woman who holds a power she is not sure is a blessing or a curse. But she knows she wants to pass it on to her unborn son no matter what.

"Cross That Bridge" brings us back to Detective Enora Palmer as she pairs up with a reluctant Detective Ponti, who has an unusual gift for finding missing children (see, he was born with an extraordinary power after all). Max Ponti tries to help this little girl as she says, 'Sometimes I just want to be someplace enough. Daddy says it's bad to want something that much.'

These characters are not easily forgotten and their stories are compelling—they resonate and live on with you, leave you asking questions. What *is* the Grey Institute anyway, and what happens to the damaged people who go there? And why are there so many different kinds of powers? This collection is sure to provide a lot of pleasure to the reading public—I know I can't wait to find out where Biancotti goes next.

Ann VanderMeer

Shades of Grey

Grey was a man who liked to plan. But right now his animal brain was taking over. His pulse raced. His stomach was twisted with adrenalin. He fancied he could feel each cell in every part of his body. He filled his lungs and sat and stared at the concrete barriers in front of him. Those foamy, rubbery things, duck-footed and already crumbling at the top edges. Five identical barriers in a row with the sky pressed flat above them and beyond an irresistible chance at personal oblivion.

He revved the engine. 'I wanted to know...'

No one to hear him, but still he practised out loud an answer to a question which—should he live—would be inevitable.

Mr Grey, why would a man of your evident wealth and standing attempt suicide in such a strange and public way? Did you need an audience for your, shall we say, swan dive into oblivion?

'No.' That was beneath him. 'Those barriers, you see? They looked just like stairs.'

It was only then, roleplaying the what-comes-after, that

he realised he was serious. He drummed his thumbs on the steering wheel. A string of stunted teeth, that's what the barriers looked like. And behind them, nothing, space, nothing. Sunlight and air, blue sky and the occasional suburban office or apartment building spread out and squatting no more than four storeys tall. He hadn't, in fact, planned this. A fact that shocked and thrilled him. Hadn't planned his visit to the building site, the slow spin of his car upwards to the top of the car park. He'd thought simply to check the progress of the work. A solid hanger of concrete and steel near a shopping mall. Solid, of course, except for the barriers. The proper girders were to come, he'd been told, the work was not yet done.

'Not finished, Mr Grey, don't want you t'get the wrong idea.'

'Just a look,' Grey had promised the site manager, and smiled and slipped a couple of fifties into the man's hand.

There was really no doubt that Grey would drive his Audi R8 Quattro to the top of the construction if he chose. He owned it, after all. And most of the buildings around it. But there was something soothing about money to most people, and Grey liked to grease a few paths in his ascent heaven-ward. He handed the man another fifty 'for the boys'.

Now, alone in his car, he gazed at the barriers. What was a man to do? Bold stripes of blue paint and even bolder smears of black rubber on their wide feet (testament, he assumed, to the attempts by others to push through those suppos-edly rigid boundaries, to spin off the edge and glide into Nietzsche's promised void).

Mr Grey? ... Why?

They'd obviously been used before on other building sites or other accidents, other attempts to seek annihilation in the face of those chunky city buoys.

'I wanted to know what it would feel like. I wanted to see ... to see how long I could keep going. If I could soar over the glass and stone suburb in a wingless machine.' Here he gave the dashboard a smooth pat. 'I wanted to make eye contact with the office workers trapped in their cubicles, faces slack with wonder...'

But here he ran out of analogy and stared, instead, at those insipid barriers. It wasn't an answer he was forming, it was an excuse. He raised his chin, squared his shoulders to the windscreen. Esser Grey didn't make excuses. He had one more go at the truth.

'I wanted to die.'

And with the irresistible fact of his desire, something inside him was quelled. He pressed his foot to the accelerator and shot towards the edge of the car park, in a car that could accelerate from nought to eighty in forty-five seconds. In one minute, he estimated, he would be soaring grille-first into the sky or dragging those barriers over the edge in an inhospitable descent.

The Audi smoothly rushed forward with minimal pressure from Grey. It connected with the barriers and pushed them out into the air in an almost straight line for what felt like minutes. Like a cartoon character hanging out over a crevasse. Then they fell, the car following its concrete partners down and down and down.

***

He felt his thumbs break first under the weight of his torso as the seat shoved him forward. He felt his ribs impact spine, hips dislocate, legs crack in half high at his thigh. He felt his neck snap as his forehead slammed into glass, nose shattering, cheekbones snapping. He bit off his tongue and broke his jaw on the exploding dashboard. Then there was the squelch of his organs, muscles pierced and compressed, everything flattening and stopping cold, all of this in a roar like the world was erupting, noise everywhere.

And then, blessed darkness. An absolute nothing that was almost a return to the womb. He sensed it rather than felt it, became it for that brief moment of overwhelming relief.

The car rocked, upside-down, groaning like an injured thing. Grey reflected that surely in death, the mind must stop working. And yet, he could hear screams and voices, faint but certainly audible. He could feel the car rock like a cradle and become still. He could feel, after a moment, the healing, stinging march through his body as it rebuilt itself.

No.

Only one thing had ever denied itself to Grey and that was death. And now, turned to paste in his destroyed car, he began to realise that the absence of death may be a permanent thing. He was a man used to getting what he wanted and to have this one thing taken away from him, well. It was unbearable.

***

No.

He tried to scream but all that came out was a gurgle of bloody phlegm.

'Jesus, mate, you okay?' A stranger's voice. The eternal question.

No.

From somewhere in the distance, someone was calling his name. Not the voice of God, he quickly surmised, but the near-hysterical shouts of his site manager. Should have slipped him another fifty to shut him up. Grey's body knitted itself back into a loose semblance of its usual shape until he was able to take a lungful of air and release it in an agonising scream at once comforting and alien.

'No!'

His newly re-formed limbs trembled, his gut emptied air and muck onto the roof below him. To his embarrassment, people ran to his aid thinking him a victim of the strange and savage event.

'Stay away from me!'

Hands reached for him. Strangers, trying to help. The very people who—until then—had probably run from the onslaught of his vehicle toppling from the sky. Once more returned to life, his hoped-for release from the press of humanity—even his own humanity—was cut off in its prime. Grey was ashamed. He wondered if this was how the gods felt, so removed from cause and effect they were, in essence, trapped. Forced to live alongside a population that drew further away the more their own godhead was revealed.

'Mr Grey! Mr Grey, are you okay?'

'No. I'm—'

But he didn't know what he was.

'There are two kinds of people with lawyers on tap, Mr Grey.'

'There are?'

He was upright, clean, in bandages and borrowed clothes but to a large extent uninjured. It was, he was sorry to say, a kind of miracle. He leaned forward, steepling his fingers, ignoring the pure bland surrounds of Botany Bay police station. Nothing in this room, for instance, but a table and three chairs, a camera high on the wall. And the detective, easing into a chair opposite him and behind a low table.

'The powerful,' she said, 'and the corrupt.'

Grey chuckled as if she'd made a joke. 'Thank you.'

'For implying you're powerful?'

'For imagining,' he countered with a deferential nod, 'that those are two different groups.'

She was young, dark-skinned, hair lacquered, hands laid now square and squarely in front of her so they formed a triangle with the base of her narrow neck. Her suit was so cheap the cloth shone at elbow and collar. Her notebook was in front of her but she hadn't touched it.

'What was your name again?' Grey asked.

'Detective Palmer,' she said without missing a beat. 'And you, Samuel Rainer Grey—'

'Please, call me Esser.'

She reflected. 'As in, your initials, Mr Grey?'

'Please,' he confirmed. 'I prefer the name I chose myself.'

She turned back to her notes. 'Let's talk about what happened today. Mister Grey.'

Ah, here it was. She would be looking for the answer. He leaned back in his chair.

'What made you do it?'

'*Made* me?' Grey echoed.

This wasn't quite the question he'd planned for. He'd long forgotten to think of himself as someone *made* to do anything by either compulsion or constraint. But if she was asking what brought him here, what had built and fashioned him into the man he'd become—what had, in effect, made him—well, that was an epistemological question worth asking. The pioneering son of pioneering parents, he liked to think every pearl had its grit, every achievement its itch. For Grey, that itch was his own parents. Where they had built houses, he built hotels. Where they funded schools, he traded in hospitals. Their offices became his city complexes, their charity work, his all-encompassing full birth-to-death life subsidies.

His charities weren't random. They were the end result of his research into the pitfalls of the human race. And his own yearning to be part of it. He groped for the answer that, hours before, had made so much sense. But something about her square gaze and the no-nonsense way she dressed made him doubt himself. Another new experience in an over-long day.

'I built that car park. Well, paid for it to be built, at least,' he stalled.

'Yes?'

'But … who designed it, I wonder? A car park over a busy shopping mall. Doesn't that seem irresponsible?'

She didn't blink. 'You think *that* was irresponsible?'

'It's an invitation to crime, isn't it?' he gestured with a hand, trying to get the explanation out. 'There we all are, pressed together into this city. And there's a precipice over which one is practically obliged to drive one's car—'

'Precipice? You mean, the car park?'

'I mean,' he confirmed, 'the car park.'

'The car park, with the solid one-foot concrete barrier along its edges?'

'I hate to disagree,' he said, 'since we've come so far. But the concrete isn't that solid. It's really the steel girders that hold the structure together. The concrete is more visual than actual deterrence, you understand. And concrete, of course, can rot. Whereas steel—'

'Let me ask again. What *made* you,' she stabbed the table with one long finger, 'drive your car *(stab)* over the edge of an Eastgardens car park *(stab)* and straight down into a busy shopping mall, ultimately injuring—directly or indirectly—no less than seventeen people *(stab)*?'

'I'm not sure I understand the question. Perhaps I'm reading too much into it.'

The detective regarded him with a steady gaze. Grey gave her a slow squint in return, gauging her. She was relaxed. Filling in time, waiting the few more minutes it would take his lawyer to arrive, knowing none of it was going to stick. Not to a man like Esser Grey.

She regrouped. 'Let's try something else. When they dragged you out of the car, you were covered in blood.'

'Yes?'

'Yet you were largely unhurt.'

'Detective,' he gave her a bruised look. 'I assure you, I do hurt.'

Alas, was she moving away from epistemology so soon?

'But how did you survive?'

'A miracle.'

'You could have killed someone.'

'I didn't.'

'Another miracle?' He could see her wondering whether to pursue his crime or his supernatural escape. 'Does that make what you did any better?'

His lawyer burst through the door in a fit of authoritarian efficiency.

'Bill,' said Grey, raising a casual hand towards his opponent, 'this is Detective … I'm so sorry?'

'Palmer,' she said, not reaching for Bill's offered hand.

'William Everton-Warburton.' Bill thumped his briefcase on the table. 'Mr Grey is a great humanitarian. He's funded hospitals, for God's sake. Charities for fertility, teen suicide, depression, child care, aged care—'

'Bill, I'm pleading guilty.'

That sparked her up. Detective Palmer even went so far as to give him a sidelong stare.

Bill adjusted without pause. 'That's exactly what I'd expect someone to say who was temporarily insane owing to … for example, the stress of his illustrious position.'

He was an implacable player, Bill. With a thick veneer of implosive outrage covering a world-weary indifference. According to Bill, he'd lived in this city for fifty of his fifty-eight years. He'd seen everything, done very little of it himself, and was used to difficult clients making difficult demands. Already he'd be calculating the cost of Grey's defence.

'I'm not insane, or stressed,' Grey said.

Bill looked pointedly at his client, then turned the same look to the detective. For a moment, nobody moved. There were just the three of them and the walls and the desk and the camera.

'Give us a moment, would you, detective,' Bill said.

Palmer moved to leave. When she walked, she held her shoulders back like a dancer, a thick plait of hair hanging halfway down her back, unswinging.

'What's this about, then, Sam?' Bill took the detective's seat. 'They allowed you access to a doctor, right? We can sue if they didn't.'

Grey almost chuckled. 'They treated me fine. Even tried to put me in a hospital. I refused.'

'Good. That sounds crazy,' said Bill approvingly. 'Those your clothes, dear boy?'

'They were lent to me. My own were caked in blood.'

'Whose? And remember, I'm your lawyer, bound by oath.'

Grey took a breath. 'Bill, I have something important to say.'

'I don't doubt it, old friend.'

'Look at this.'

Grey raised his arms to reveal minor scratches on his knuckles and arms which, even now, were developing a thin pink skein of healing. He unwound the bandage on his elbow like a serpent. The last few layers were hard with dried blood, but underneath was a narrow, uneven cut across his forearm, scabbed over and healing fast.

'Those your only injuries?' Bill asked.

'Everything else has already healed.'

'Airbags worked? We could sue Audi,' Bill asked.

'I had the airbags disabled some months ago.'

'Good grief, why?'

Grey ran a manicured fingernail along the uneven edge of the desk. He resented the world's attempts to soften its edges.

'Seven months ago, my birthday—'

'That was some party.'

'Quite. I'm afraid, though, I took it upon myself to drive home.'

'I won't ask how inebriated you were.'

'Very.'

Bill waved a hand. 'I should've said, don't *tell* me how inebriated you were.'

'No one died, Bill. Least of all me, though I did my best to.'

'My boy, did you attempt suicide?' Bill looked aghast.

'No. That is, not purposefully. Not that time.'

The car had pinwheeled twice over the side of a bridge and struck an embankment, rolling to its side with Grey so thoroughly wedged into his seat by the airbags he hadn't even been able to reach his phone. Transfixed by the car's mandatory safety features, Grey felt the beginnings of this new budding resentment. Surely the law had no right to ensure his safety, not in the face of his own overwhelming desire for destruction?

Much later he wondered how he'd come to escape without a scratch when the car had been written off. He'd attributed it, at the time, to the unwitting luck of drunks. The seatbelt-shaped bruise faded minutes after his escape and the cut on his neck—so deep it whistled when he breathed—was gone by morning.

He wondered if that's how it had begun, whether his strange power had started then. Or perhaps he had just never died before.

'The airbags,' he said, 'bothered me.'

'You don't have to play it up with me, Sam. We'll get you the insanity plea.'

'You're not seeing it, Bill. I can't be injured. I've tried countless times since then and I ... heal.'

Bill shifted his weight to sit side-on to Grey. He hooked an elbow over the back of his chair and crossed his legs. All the while he sighed and frowned. 'So what are we saying here?'

'Today I died.'

'You blacked out.'

'No. Truly died. Bill, what does it mean? What if I can

never die? Will I be the only man to live forever?'

Bill squirmed, looking uncomfortable. 'The world's a big, busy place, Sam, with more wonders… Ah, hell, who can say? My mother taught me it's arrogance to think we're unique. A trick of the ego.'

'Of course,' Grey felt chastised.

'Let's talk about your defence, old friend.'

'I want to go to prison and do my time.'

'Ah!' Bill threw up his hands. 'Good heavens, why?'

Cause and effect, Grey thought. *Desire and consequence.* He wanted to go to prison because he deserved it. Because when people did bad things, that's where they went. People who, like him, had run out of caring for self and others. 'I put people in danger.'

'Clearly you're contrite, that will stand you in good stead.'

'I'm serious.'

'Sam,' Bill sighed, 'prison is a dry existence. Same four walls every day, same narrow bed, same rather bland attire. Hell, same food, I wouldn't wager. Imagine the rest of your life in a room like this one.' He gestured at the wall and table and camera. 'Whatever's going on in your head, prison's not going to make it better.'

'You've no idea, Bill, what it's like,' Grey's voice was quiet. 'Detached from the threat—the opportunity—of death. Everything that lives should die. Bill? Don't you agree? I want to be judged by my peers, I want…'

He had to pause, to still the shake in his voice and the unaccustomed emotion pressing on his throat. He wanted to know what he was. He wanted to be part of something he understood. Was he, indeed, part of the human race? Or something else? Some nascent god with a taste for destruction?

'So we plead guilty, old boy, and go straight to prison. Or we plead innocent by reason of diminished capacity.'

'I'm doing it alone this time. I intend to go to prison, and I don't want to drag you down with me. I'll defend myself.'

Bill was thoughtful. He tapped a fingernail against his lips, sighed and rose from his chair. 'I hate to see you do this. But it goes against the grain, friend, to try helping someone who doesn't want the help. And besides, it doesn't do my business any good.'

'I knew you'd understand,' Grey smiled.

'Oh, I wouldn't say that,' Bill muttered. 'But good luck with it. It's a far, far nobler thing you do. And so on.'

'Bill?'

'Yes?'

Grey held up his forearm—his perfect, clean, healed forearm—and showed that where the jagged scab had been was now pale skin glowing with health.

'Good Lord,' said Bill. 'Good Lord.'

His voice was soft with wonder. He gripped Grey's hand and held it tight.

After Bill left, the detective came to take his place. She had something about her, Grey noted. A way of walking that tied the casual stroll with a purposeful stride but came up in between. She slapped a folder on the table and stooped, not quite sitting.

He'd forgotten her name again.

She looked from the unravelled bandages to Grey's smooth arms and a light went on in her eyes.

'Your injuries. They've healed.' It wasn't a question.

Grey smiled. 'What injuries?'

He spread his hands wide as if in flight. As if in a long, spiralling descent.

'You're representing yourself?' asked the judge.

Grey indicated to his left the empty chairs, the upturned glasses beside the pitcher of water.

'I have to ask,' the judge said.

'I understand,' Grey nodded and smiled like he was conducting a business meeting.

'Seems unusual, a man in your position.'

The judge was a frowning man. He looked like someone who cared. About everything, even little things. He made it look exhausting. Deep grooves had earned a permanence on his skin.

'You've heard of me?' Grey asked.

'Who hasn't?' The judge glanced at the papers in front of him. 'Not guilty, is it?'

'It is, for now.'

'Is it or isn't it?' the judge asked churlishly.

Grey did a quick calculation. Bill had said his best bet for prison was to plead not guilty.

'Is,' he smiled.

The judge flipped through papers. Here, in the court-room, his future in balance, he was invigorated. The sense of impending consequence and limited possibility, this was what most people felt most of the time. A delicate vulnerability and robust sense of *minutiae*. Everything mattered. Everything was extraordinary. The grain of wood under his hands, the angle of his seat, the height of the judge's desk, the tinge of stuffiness in the room. None of it would ever be this way again. The judicial process had been designed by humanity to hold and guide life and death decisions and he—Esser Grey—was deep in its womb. He was, for the first time, part of something.

The judge said, 'Trial to commence at the earliest convenience.'

He banged a gavel on his desk, making a hollow, almost meek sound. Like a child clapping.

The trial was less straightforward than Grey expected. He reminded himself that the business of business was remarkably different to the business of law.

'State your name for the record,' the court official intoned.

God, that man could sing marvellous opera if he wanted. Grey would try to ask him later if he had any ambitions outside his work—which was, admittedly, a fairly low-grade sort of affair.

'Samuel Rainer Grey.'

'Place your left hand on the Bible.'

Grey hesitated. It was hard to believe in God when one felt one might *be* a god. He went through the motions and sat smoothly under the weight of the stares from the entire room. Families and victims were easy to spot. They travelled in packs and glared with wet fury. Media was also simple. Something had sucked the soul out of journalism long ago, leaving behind a postmodern jadedness that wrestled with its traditional self-righteousness. Plus they carried pens. The rest were tourists, of a kind. People looking for a place to exercise their sense of moral outrage.

The prosecutor approached, drawing the future with her. 'Mr Grey, tell me what happened that day.'

When it was over thirty-eight days later, Grey rose when asked and turned to the jury. He held his hands behind his back to give the impression of being receptive and ready. The head jurist was a portly man with a bald patch like a Benedictine monk's. He wore a brown suit that might have fitted him once, but now hung narrow off his shoulders while his white-shirted belly protruded like frosted pudding.

'How,' asked the judge with his customary frown, 'do you find?'

The portly man cleared his throat, rocked unsteadily on his feet, and held onto a piece of paper like he was using it to steer.

'On the count of reckless endangerment, we find the defendant guilty.'

Ahh, that's the ticket, Grey thought, relaxing.

'On the twenty-three counts of attempted manslaughter, we find the defendant … not guilty.'

The judge accepted the verdict matter-of-factly. 'Thank you. The jury is dismissed.'

Hold on, hold on, *what was happening?* Grey raised a hand, compelling the room to silence. He fixed his gaze on the portly jurist.

'I'm sorry, could you read that again?'

'Mr Grey—'

'Your Honour, I don't understand.'

'Mr Grey, I believe the finding is one of diminished responsibility.'

No.

The crowd growled and somewhere to his right Grey thought he heard Bill's distinctive hacking laugh.

'It means you're not deemed responsible for your actions,' the judge explained.

'Then who on earth do you believe more thoroughly responsible for my actions?'

'This is merely a courtroom, Mr Grey. Not your psychiatrist's office. But, to the point. What matters is that the punishment fit the crime. And since your intentions towards the crime are … uncertain … it would be remiss of the judicial system to allow you to go to prison. You are helpless to help yourself, Mr Grey. As a responsible society, we must step in.'

'You,' said Grey, '*are* kidding, aren't you?'

The judge wasn't kidding. Grey was released not even to some helpful institution (despite suggestions from the judiciary) but ultimately to house arrest. The media joked that though his city apartment was certainly big enough for an average-sized prison, as it housed only one prisoner it was somewhat excess to requirements. Also his harbour view was unlike any found in prisons anywhere.

For Grey it was the most disappointing defeat he could have imagined. Here in his apartment he was just as isolated as ever. He could no longer see the city in close-up, its oil-and-tyre stained muck collected along its kerbs. Here he saw the ocean and the green of aged fig trees in parkland and the distant swarm of humanity. Here he felt nothing.

He briefly tried cutting himself. He found a grim satisfaction in visiting these temporary damages on his body. Suicide, previously a one-off option, now obsessed him. But at worst his attempts to die left him more alienated than before. Throwing himself from the building, he knew from his car park experience, wouldn't work. So his attention quickly turned instead to poisons, easily procurable from online sources. He was able to effect stomach aches and other symptoms, at one point suffering all his hair falling out and the yellowing of his previously manicured nails.

He healed and healed. In frustration he dashed the poison bottles against the kitchen floor. And then, embarrassed, he scraped and cleaned up all the pieces, lest his housekeeper find them and cut herself on poisoned glass. On his knees on the kitchen tiles, he cursed himself for his absurdity, ignoring the cuts on his fingers until his blood made the glass too slippery to grasp.

'Look at you. You're a danger to others, you foolish—'

He had an idea. He'd been thinking of his strange power as a curse, but what if it was something else? What if it was some kind of blessing? A recognition of the good way he'd tried to live his life in the face of all the temptations of his privilege. If that was the case, then there was a way to slip free of this damned blessing's hold, to cease living apart. To rejoin the human race. And that was to commit another, more serious crime. Something unaccountable, inescapable, and horrific.

The idea both tantalised and, briefly, terrified him.

For the task he chose someone much closer to home (as it had to be, given his incarceration). Live-in help was an old-fashioned thing, and besides he'd grown if not attached to, then impressed by, his housekeeper. He dismissed her immediately and began advertising for just the right person. Subservient, hollow, someone with a complete lack of spirit.

The men he interviewed generally mistook his intentions and the women declined to live in a man's prison. Most of the applicants were too young, too full of promise and plans. He needed someone who wouldn't miss life. When he found the perfect weak-souled individual, he discouraged her from sharing even her name. He paid cash in generous amounts and asked her to keep to herself.

She was plain and long-limbed, with a penchant for polish on her toenails. She spoke little, which helped, and kept good house, which didn't. She appeared to have little in the way of friends or family, which Grey understood too keenly. Even Bill hadn't been to visit him since the trial. He resolved to act quickly.

In the early morning dark, he went to her room. She slept with her curtains open, he noticed, all the lights of the city bleeding in. He crossed silently to the bed. In her somnambulant state, she left him no space to slip the scarf under her neck, and he was forced to use his hands—bare, as they were, against her bare neck. The heat and pulse of her throat disgusted him, and he had to lean harder and harder into his thumbs to cut off her gurgling cries.

Her eyes rolled open and she watched him with a terrible mix of horror and fatalism, her hands doing little to loosen his grip. He recognised in her a desire to die, and that shocked him because, until then, he'd been careful not to relate to her. And here she was, forcing him to acknowledge the very thing that united them the most. Grey cursed her as he killed her, his spittle marking her face and his tears finally blurring the sight of her stare.

Something snapped in her neck and the woman shuddered hard enough to rock the bed. Even then she stank of skin and heat.

Grey's stomach clenched. He stormed to her bathroom and vomited into the toilet, an act and a setting that caused him even greater disgust. He did not fail to note the messy collection of talc and perfume and other slippery tools of personal grooming embellishing every bathroom surface. He felt the weight of the woman's life then. Her unmet potential, the erasure of every promise she'd ever had cause to receive or make. He felt, to his surprise, disgusted with himself and kind of small. An almost insignificant agent in the sequence that had served to overwhelm and undermine this woman's life.

He'd planned, after the crime, to return to his hoard of poison and blades, to test out his theory. To see if the removal of the blessing was complete. He'd planned it, but when the moment came to cross her room and back out through her door, in the dark, with only the distant city lights to guide him, he found himself afraid.

'I wanted,' he said, 'to see…'

And here he found himself sobbing, crouched over a stranger's toilet gripping the porcelain like it might save him from whatever he'd become. A monster. A murderer. Dawn found him there an hour later: a tiny, staring man in a broad apartment in a building crowding the edge of the salt water that edged, in turn, the city. His city, with its load of alien humanity. A man who might have been a god who had surely become the devil. He felt, at last, tethered to the world. Not floating free above it. He had a sensation that was equal parts relief and dread.

The next trial was much more brief.

Institutionalised at last, his first visitor was a cop. Not just any cop, but the detective, the one who'd been there at the start.

'Detective Palmer,' he said, recognising at once her strong hands and the creamy dark of her skin. 'Well, well. And is your interest purely prurient? I wouldn't blame you, of course.'

She sat opposite him. No glass dividers for Grey, no maximum security, high density prison. He was still deemed too helpless, crazed, a victim of his own insanity.

'I wanted to see if you could still heal yourself in a place designed to destroy little by little. Mr Grey?'

'Would you believe…' He leaned forward and rolled up his sleeve, revealing the smooth, almost hairless skin of his upper arm. 'Do you like my tattoos? The inmates gave them to me. I won't show you where else they tried to scar me. Even fully healed it isn't a sight for polite company.'

Palmer regarded the blank slate of his bicep. 'So you can.'

'I'm afraid so.'

'"Afraid" is surely the wrong word. You can't be afraid of anything, with all your wealth and—'

'Power?'

'That's it,' she smiled, but sadly. As if she might be sorry for him. 'I think I know what you're doing.'

'And what is that?'

She laced her fingers so her hands, joined, resembled a hammer head, a blunt axe. 'You're our terrible warning.'

Grey laughed, throwing his head back. Above him the ceiling was the colour of gun metal. The walls were gun metal, too, and so was the floor. In every part of the building the windows seemed far away. They felt like they belonged to different walls and looked out on different worlds that had nothing to do with the right-here, right-now.

It soothed him.

'I aimed at no such thing, Detective.'

'I think you wanted to show everyone what happens when someone tries to throw himself away.'

Grey still had a smile on his face. It was one of the few freedoms left to him. 'And what is it, exactly, that happens when one tries to throw oneself away?'

Palmer's knuckles were like bolts, jutting from the backs of her hands.

'Someone catches you,' she said. 'You drive off a roof, you're given the benefit of the doubt. You murder a young woman in your employ. You're put in a mental asylum.'

'It *is* a prison,' he told her gently.

'Sure it is. And you're a wealthy man. You've probably already bought it.'

Grey spoke quickly. 'You're one of the few people left who doesn't see me as a monster.'

'Oh, I wouldn't say that, Mr Grey, we're all monsters. But you can't let what you *are* define you.'

She moved to leave and Grey felt an absurd desire to stay her. He reached out and took hold of her wrist, his thumb pressed to its soft underside.

'I hope I can look forward to hearing more from you, Detective. And finding a way to repay your faith in me.'

'Coming from a committed murderer, that should probably make me nervous.'

'Didn't you hear? I'm reformed.' Suddenly aware of the warmth of her skin, he let his hand drop. '"Every living thing must die", Detective. Do you know which philosopher said that?'

'I don't. But if I get to Heaven, I'll ask around.'

'You see? This is my question. If I can't die, can I get to heaven?'

Palmer leaned forward. 'If you can't die, maybe you'll find something valuable to do down here.'

'Like?'

'Helping other people like you. Maybe,' she shrugged. 'Or people not like you. Or, whoever comes your way.'

Grey was thoughtful. 'Detective. There's some intelligence to that idea.'

'Yeah, I have hidden depths. And thank you.'

'For acknowledging your intelligence?'

Palmer raised her hand in a mock salute, 'For remembering my name.'

Grey watched her go, leaving him alone in his gun metal room. It wasn't like he could stop her. He was wedged between the walls, sandwiching his life choices into the spaces and shapes allowed him by the rest of his human inmates. This place hadn't destroyed him either, and he wondered just how long a life sentence could outlast even his unblemished life. He found the prospect soothing.

Palming the Lady

'That woman is stalking me.'

Detective Palmer eased forward, looking along the young man's arm to where he pointed through the window.

'*That* woman?' she indicated, to be sure.

Outside, the dusty light hung on the thick city air. Solid in the middle of the crowd, one woman stood out. Heavyset, old, with a round flat face like a moon, she stood and stared at the apartment where Palmer and the young man stood. It was a warm day, but she was wearing a long dirty sweater and thick skirt over tights. She looked homeless.

'Yes! Her, *her!*' Matthew Webb stabbed the air with all four fingers clenched, palm flat. 'I've moved house three times. She turns up at my front door—'

'You leave a forwarding address?'

'No! Sorry, Detective,' Matthew collected himself. 'My mail goes to my parents' house.'

'Are they near here?'

'No. Hunters Hill, other side of the bridge.'

Palmer liked to think she took people on a case-by-case basis. So she tucked aside the prejudice that arose from his privileged address. She estimated a homeless woman on foot would take a couple of hours each direction to get from Ultimo to Hunters Hill. And this woman wasn't fit. Her arms stuck out at her sides to accommodate her bulk. So, half a day. And then she'd have to get back.

'And she's not anyone you know?'

'Hell no! No, sorry.'

Seemed like Webb had his own prejudices.

Palmer straightened. Shoulders back, hands clasped loosely behind her, expression—she hoped—attentive. She poised with her pen over her notebook to show she was listening. In conducting interviews, she had a plain, non-accusatory style that had previously earned commendations from her command. Her boss told her she 'accepted people on their own terms'. More informally, he said she 'did good with the crazies'. 'You're good at the whole compassion thing,' he liked to tell her, in a tone that made it clear he considered that an insult. So Palmer had become a one-woman travelling unit for all of the city's worst nuttiness.

'Let's recap. That woman there, outside, follows you from apartment to apartment, lecture to lecture.'

'She's there before me. Like she knows where I'll be before I do. She knows when I go to the library, she knows where I go to lunch. If my dad would let me quit this stupid degree … I think I'm going crazy, you know?'

Crazy. That word meant something to Palmer. She spent longer than lighter-skinned people trying to appear just right. Walk and talk just right, smile and think just right.

There was nothing like faking normal to send a person crazy. She checked her notes.

'Medical degree. Following in your father's footsteps?'

Matthew nodded. His shoulders were slumped. He ran a hand through his hair. 'Can you help me?'

He held both hands out like a penitent. Palmer would remember that about him later. She felt herself softening.

'I'll talk to her. But stalking isn't illegal in this State. And if she hasn't done anything threatening,' she spread her hands, thumbs out, 'there's not much I can do.'

'Just one day free of that freak.'

The signs of wear were in his face. The tics at the edge of his mouth, the way the skin around his eyes was pulled taut. His gaze had that dull patina peculiar to the hunted. What she didn't understand was why a homeless woman would track—even could track—a young medical student from an apparently well-to-do family.

'I can probably do that,' she said, making the only promise she could.

Wedged between the CBD and Sydney University, Ultimo mixed an impoverished student population with the over-spill of inner city fashionistas. Despite that, something about Ultimo felt old and dangerous. Crowded apartment blocks leaned over historic pubs and churches. Three fires had struck the suburb in the past year. They all had explanations, but after three, explanations had begun to sound like excuses.

Leaving Webb's apartment and crossing the street, all Palmer's senses were on edge. Like she was walking into a boxing ring. She eyed the strange woman and the woman, in turn, watched her with a sharp stare. There was no doubt about it, this woman was homeless. Her long grey hair was matted and her clothes filthy. Her arms swung at her sides with pendulous certainty, forward and back. Forward and back. Where the woman's fingers emerged from her multiple sweaters, they were thin and childlike, the skin shining red. Her dull pink sweater showed another, darker pullover below its hemline, and she was rotund as a damn barrel through the chest. Palmer sweated into her shirt just looking at her.

'I'm Detective Palmer,' she held up a Central Metro badge. 'What's your name?'

'Got the time?' the woman countered.

Palmer checked her watch. 'Eleven-oh-five.'

The woman chewed this over. 'It's a little late.'

'It usually is. You need to be someplace?'

'Prince Alfred's.'

'The hospital? You need a ride?'

'Nah, I know the backstreets.'

'They expecting you?'

'They feed me.'

'They know your name?'

'Barely know it myself.'

The woman had large flat eyes and she stank of street living. Oils and dust and the detritus of human consumption that had been trapped and allowed to ferment in her too-many sweaters. Palmer breathed shallowly.

'Well, what did your mother call you?'

'She never called,' her arms swung higher. 'She's been gone a long time. Maybe forever.'

'Dead?'

'Guess so. When I think of her, I see dark. Been that way for as long as I can remember.'

Palmer flipped out her notebook. The sun cut grooves into her neck where her collar finished, and she had to fan herself with one hand for relief from the heat. Not a breeze to speak of here under the heavy skyline.

'I want to ask you about the young man you've been following.'

A flat, affronted glare from the woman. 'Haven't been following him.'

'No?'

Clockwise and back went the woman's arms, clockwise and back. The movement someone might make in a cold bath, pushing the water around for warmth. 'Where's your partner?'

Palmer hesitated. 'Detectives can work without partners.'

'They send a detective to do an officer's job?' the woman asked with startling clarity.

She was spinning those arms higher, sending her unwashed stink into the air. A little higher and Palmer could get slapped. Assaulting an officer. Useful charge to get someone off the street for a day.

'You understand something about policing?' Palmer asked.

'I understand something about timing. I've seen your future.'

'How's that?'

The woman shrugged, inclining her flat face towards her collarbone. 'It's my gift. Your partner's in the hospital.'

Palmer didn't find much in life that frightened her. She'd given up on scary movies when she was ten, she'd given up on scary boyfriends sometime after that. Police work might've put her in danger a few times, but it wasn't frightening. Even the hospital guess (spot on, though it undeniably was) didn't scare her. What the crazy old woman with the pendulum arms said next, now that scared her.

'He's not going to forgive you.'

Palmer went cold. 'How do you know that?'

She'd meant it to sound light, sarcastic. But it didn't.

'Told you. I got a gift.'

Palmer pressed her fingers so hard to the pen an ache started in her wrist. She felt the edges of her mouth pull out and down into a rictus. Like the time she'd found Tim O'Donnell lying behind a back fence, bullet wounds bleeding out through his favourite suit. No sign of the shooter. No way for Palmer to explain to the investigators why she hadn't been at his side. *Partnerships were like marriage*, O'Donnell liked to say. He should know, he'd been through a few. Now he was in hospital and Palmer was pulling the menial jobs and the weird stuff nobody else cared about.

'I've got some questions for you,' she told the woman, 'down the station.'

The woman smirked toothlessly. What small eyes she had disappeared into loose pockets of flesh. 'I know.'

***

Newtown Police Station was in an unassuming street with the assuming name of Australia Street. Two doors south was a pub. One street east was the pink art deco hulk of an ex-peep-show known as The Hub. The original tenants had been gone a couple of decades, but the red 'Hub' lettering was still there.

Newtown itself was a mess of give-and-take, just the way Palmer liked it. The pizzeria beside The Hub held a memory of an ex-lover dumping her while plucking anchovies from his Italian Supreme. Less than a block west was an Eastern trade store where she'd worked her way through university. Until a memorable police raid had confiscated illegal goods from every shelf: souvenirs of her boss's junkets to Thailand. Palmer had quit in disgust and spent three days living on stale bread before her next gig.

It gave her a grim satisfaction to pass those landmarks, even now, and feel like she was some kind of survivor. That's what she liked about the city, the sense she'd survived it.

She walked the strange woman to an interview room and watched her slow, waddling shuffle. Arms wide, feet at a shuffle, chin tucked into the folds of her neck. Palmer could feel the stares of her colleagues. *Another of Palmer's crazies*, they'd be saying. She was cursed.

They took seats opposite each other, the table between them dull with age.

'Matthew Webb,' Palmer began.

'Who?'

'The young medical student you're following.'

'Don't have to follow him,' the woman beamed, fat with pride. 'I know where he'll be.'

'Your gift.'

'That's it.'

Palmer laced her fingers on her knee, leaning back in her chair to give the woman a look of bored attention. *Impress me*, that's what her stare meant. It usually worked, and it worked that time, too. She started fidgeting, looking at the walls, the table, the camera, the window that mimicked a mirror.

'Tell me. *How* do you know where he'll be?'

'I think of him and I see him where he's going to be.'

'You ever been wrong?' Palmer asked.

'No. You?'

Palmer ignored the question. 'Where is he now?'

'Told you. I don't know now, I only know soon.'

'How soon?'

The woman shrugged. 'I got it down to five minutes sometimes.'

'So, where's he going to be *soon?*'

The woman balled her hands into fists on the table and lowered her head, beating a tattoo alternately on the table and her own forehead. Her hands were always moving. *Measuring time*, Palmer thought suddenly. Acting like a kind of grammar, dividing one moment from the next.

'A bus stop,' the woman's voice was muffled behind her long hair. 'Broadway Road. Going to the city.'

Palmer checked her watch and made a note on the pad in her lap. 'What's your name?'

'Don't need one. No one much talks to me, I don't much talk to no one.'

'We're talking, right?'

'So what're you calling me?'

Contrary Mary, that's what leapt into Palmer's mind. Contrary Mary, the nickname they'd given her aunt before the suicide. Palmer pushed the memory away.

The woman chuckled. No reason for it, just laughed like she'd heard a joke. Palmer slapped her notepad hard on the table to silence her. Mary jumped, hands flexing. The blank shine left her eyes, and when it left there was nothing but darkness.

'You can see the future?' Palmer leaned forward. 'That what you're saying?'

'Mostly the future, yeah. Never done good with the past. Maybe like you, Detective?'

'Matthew Webb,' Palmer's voice was stern.

'The boy, yeah, you said.'

'Why do you show up at his house? Why do you go to his classes? Why do you follow him?'

Mary turned her stare to her lap, muttering something Palmer couldn't hear.

'Speak up!'

Mary lifted her chin so high her flat face was almost heavenward. 'I said I like the shine of his skin.'

Palmer paused. 'That's it?'

Mary grinned again, gums red and empty. 'And he's big news. In the future, he's famous. He's got a cure.'

'For what?'

'I dunno. Something big. Maybe cancer, maybe death. Hey, maybe he'll cure death?' Mary rolled her eyes like she was searching.

Palmer felt herself flinch. She thought briefly of O'Donnell and then pushed the idea aside. 'That'd be something, a cure for death. How's he get this cure?'

'Research, I suppose. When he's sixty, maybe more, he's getting prizes all over the place. Isn't that something, Detective? Gives you hope, hey.'

Hope.

'You can see his entire future?'

'Got no need for all that. Just need to know where he's going to be today. But sometimes I look too far, and there he is when he's sixty, seventy.'

'You recognise him?'

'I'm not stupid.'

'You see everyone's futures?'

A shrug. 'Not all at once. But one at a time, if I concentrate real hard. Yeah.'

'You see my future?'

Mary pulled on her lower lip. 'You wouldn't like it.'

'Try me.'

She started small. What Palmer would have for dinner two nights from now (soup, apparently, no surprises there), a new job she'd get a bunch of years from now, the name of her 'next partner'. Palmer raised a hand to cut her off, but too slowly.

Mary tapped one hand against another. 'That O'Donnell, he's not going to forgive you.'

Palmer's gut rolled. That was Contrary Mary's real

power. It wasn't the future she traded in exactly. It was fear of the future.

'How do you know about O'Donnell?'

'You're not listening! I see the future. I see his name on a whiteboard on a hospital bed and I see them cleaning it off. He's not getting out and he's not coming back.' Her voice softened. 'We all gotta go, Detective. Well, until we got a cure for it.'

'What's your name?' Palmer croaked, voice closing down.

'Contrary Mary.'

Palmer would never forget how still the room became. Even Mary's hands stopped moving. In that insulated space, not a sound could be heard, not a breath could be taken.

'You read minds.'

'I read futures. I see it clear like it's already happened. The future's just as here and now as the present. Nothing to do but make your peace.'

'So how'd you get that name?'

'From a phone call you're gonna make, tomorrow morning, first thing.'

Palmer thought back to the student apartment in Ultimo with Matthew Webb hiding in a shadow by the window. 'You understand, you were brought here for questioning about the alleged harassment of Matthew Webb.' She paused to let Mary nod and issue a guttural 'huh'. 'I now believe you to be a potential harm to yourself and will remand you in custody for psychological assessment.'

'So what? I'll be out tomorrow.'

Exactly, thought Palmer. *Welcome to your future.*

***

The psychologist's report was compiled overnight. Palmer was at work early. Her boss, Earn Cullen, was already in the office.

'Interesting Jane Doe you've unearthed, Detective,' he called from his office.

'Yes, sir.'

'She's been regaling staff all night. Telling fortunes, I understand.'

'Don't think that's illegal, is it, sir?'

Cullen nodded his heavy chin. 'Don't know why she's taking up real estate in our cells, then. Detective.'

'No, sir.'

Jane Doe, said the report, *no fixed address*. It went on to point out the several ways Mary appeared immediately crazy ('detached from reality', the report called it, and 'prone to confabulation'), and her strange charisma.

'An ability to manipulate the emotions of her audience. Potential borderline personality disorder.'

Palmer rang the shrink, Jeffrey Andrews. 'Did I wake you?'

'It's five-thirty in the morning, what do you think?'

'This woman you interviewed last night, Contrary Mary...'

Her voice trailed off. She hadn't said the name out loud before. But just like Mary had predicted, here she was on the phone, first thing in the morning, announcing it.

'She told me your pet name for her.'

'Except I haven't called her that. Not until now.'

There was a pause as Andrews gathered himself further out of sleep. 'Okay,' he drew it out, 'so she made it up. Not unknown for a patient with—'

'No, I did call her that. I mean, just ... in my head.'

'Well,' professionally dismissive even half-asleep, 'it's possible to find ourselves convinced of something after the fact. Often the mental labels we use aren't as verbal as we think. You gave her a name mentally, she said "Contrary Mary" and you became convinced she was perceiving something unsaid. You see?'

'I know what I called her. I used that exact name. And a few minutes later she said it out loud.'

'You can't prove—'

'I can tell time, Jeff.'

Andrews' voice dropped a tone. 'I know that, Detective.'

'She told me my future.'

'She made up a fictional future for you.'

'Maybe.' Palmer couldn't explain her reaction to Mary, not in any logical way. It felt like truth. But if she told Andrews that, he'd argue it was words, not truth. As if the distinction was useful.

'She told me my future, too,' said Andrews.

'What was it?'

'In the words of Dorothy Parker—'

'I know. No one gets a happy ending.'

'You want to hear something really creepy, you should ask her what she sees in her own future.'

Palmer fingered the report in front of her.

'No, I didn't put it in the notes,' said Andrews. 'I don't

want to accuse anyone of a crime that hasn't happened.'

'She's the victim of a crime?'

'In the version she tells.'

Palmer resisted the urge to ask more. She was being reminded how much she disliked the smugness in his voice.

'I tell you, smelling that bad should be a crime,' continued Andrews. 'You know they burnt her clothes because they were worried about the public health? Bradley told me, said the pile went up like an oil pump.'

'All right, thanks.' She was about to hang up but she heard Andrews' voice from the distant phone. 'What?'

'I said, how's Tim?'

'Still in hospital. They're not optimistic.'

Andrews let out a breath. 'Poor old Tim, hey? Lived his life like he had all the time in the world. I'm s—'

But the rest was lost when she hung up.

The next person she called was Webb. Someone else answered the phone. An older voice, gruff and demanding. When she explained who she was, his voice became gruffer.

'You managed to lock up that psychopath yet, Detective? I've a mind to sue your whole department if my son doesn't receive some respite.'

'Doctor Webb, we're doing what we can.'

There was a snort, some derisive comment that was mainly inaudible. But at least he put Matthew on the phone.

'It's Detective Palmer,' she said. 'Can I ask where you were at 11.56 am yesterday? Around half an hour after I left.'

'Er, right. Um. I went into town,' said Webb.

'You caught a bus?'

'Yeah, from Broadway Road.'

'Do you still have the bus ticket?' Palmer stared at her notes.

'Um, yeah—'

'What timestamp's on it?'

Silence on the line. Then, 'Hang on.' There was a clunk as he put down the phone. He returned quickly. '11.57 am. Why, do I need an alibi, or something?'

'Nothing like that. One more question. What kind of medicine are you interested in?'

'I'm just a student—'

'You thinking of going into research, by any chance? Say, cancer? Or … something like that?'

He hesitated. His voice lowered to a whisper. 'My dad's been trying to convince me. Does that matter?'

'I don't know. No, I'm sure it doesn't. Thanks, Matthew.'

'Hey, what happened with her, though? The stalker woman?'

'She's in custody. I'm sorry, we'll have to let her go today.'

There was no mistaking the dread in his voice. 'Okay, well. I appreciate your help, Detective.'

'Sorry I couldn't do more.' She hung up before Matthew could challenge her.

Contrary Mary was cheerful that morning, and chatty. She'd slept all night in a real bed, and they'd even fed her, giving her seconds when she asked politely. She couldn't identify what she'd been eating, but that might have had as much to do with the cooking as her ignorance of modern cuisine. They'd given her new clothes. In less layers, she was smaller than anticipated, her moon-face floating above an emaciated body.

'You going to tell me your name?' Palmer asked.

'Reckon not.'

Palmer hadn't expected anything else. 'You're free to go. But if you have time, I'd appreciate you answering one more question.'

'I got time,' Mary nodded.

'If you really can see the future,' countered Palmer. 'You already know my question.'

'Ha! You beginning to believe, Detective? Knew you would. Still gotta ask, though. We all gotta keep going, else the future falls apart. See? And then where does the present go? That's our responsibility, those that know the future. Gotta protect the present.'

Palmer paused, trying to take it in. 'So, we're responsible for the future?'

Mary grinned toothlessly. 'You understand responsibility, don't you, Detective? You want to be part of the future. We all do. So, ask.'

'What you said about Tim, was it true?'

'Future's always true. Else it's not the future. Else it's a dream. That's not the end of your questions, though.'

'One more,' Palmer confirmed.

Mary nodded assent, hands flexing like claws in front of her.

'Your future?'

Those blank eyes raked Palmer. 'Big of you. You and the shrink. Most people never ask. Most people too wrapped up in themselves to take the time to listen. Always cutting people off when they're talking. You notice that?'

Palmer shrugged. 'Maybe. There's not always time—'

'Time's the only thing there is, Detective. Being in a rush doesn't change how much time you get. Future's coming anyhow,' Mary grinned with her wet, gummy mouth. 'Me, I'm gonna be part of the bigger picture.'

She didn't offer more, so Palmer asked, 'That's it?'

'That's all I'm telling you. I know how you gotta enjoy a riddle, being a detective. You work out the rest.'

She moved to leave. Palmer stayed her, reaching out to shake Mary's hand before she thought better of it. Mary—grinning like a prom queen—hesitantly took hold with both hands. Her skin was warm and soft, her palms moist.

They stood barely moving. Palmer had an absurd image of the two of them like rocks in a river, holding steady before the rush and wash of water could topple them.

Then Mary let go and Palmer had to fight the urge to rub her palm on the side of her pants.

'Thank you, Detective Palmer.'

'For what?'

Mary grinned. 'For being a part of it, too. The bigger picture. Despite yourself.'

Nodding her chin into the folds of her neck, Contrary Mary walked away, arms spinning.

'You need a ride?' Palmer called after her, but Mary didn't hear.

Palmer was to remember that moment: Mary crossing the square in front of The Hub, between the jugglers and the dog walkers. She was to wonder more than once whether it was Mary's foresight that sent her mad in the first place. And then she was to wonder where the present was really taking her. That was the problem with knowing the future. There was no way back.

Within a week Palmer knew something was wrong. Webb had moved house again, and maybe Mary had followed him because she was gone, too. Palmer took to touring hospitals and shelters, first from plain curiosity and then with increasing dread. Mary was nowhere to be found.

Cullen told her in no uncertain terms this was crazy, so she did it on her own time. Maybe it was crazy, maybe Mary had rubbed off on her.

At Prince Alfred's they hadn't seen her since before Palmer picked her up.

'So she never came in here with a new set of clothes and the grime washed off her face?'

'A clean face? No,' the nurse confirmed. 'Left with one occasionally. Bathing Mel the Bad Smell is how we break in the new recruits.'

'That your name for her?'

'Had to call her something.' The nurse smiled with a mild malice. She had the grim face too many years in medicine almost inevitably produced.

Palmer handed her several business cards. 'Hand these around, would you? If anyone sees her—'

'Sure, sure, we'll call you.'

She chased down Matthew Webb's parents at their Hunters Hill address. Despite regular water restrictions, the lawns were deep green, hedges blossoming. The house was two-storey, with balconies that were a throwback to something colonial. There was a wide-canopied tree in front just crying out for a swing or a hammock, or both. It was the kind of picturesque place you could imagine families being raised with traditional rigour. Except families largely couldn't afford this suburb anymore.

Mrs Webb opened the door, a slim woman with a wide face. She used the door for support and when she walked she swayed. Palmer put it down to a prescription problem. The rich, she'd learned, weren't immune to a desire to escape their lives. However expensive they were.

Mrs Webb showed Palmer to a wide, white lounge room where they waited for her husband to join them. She spoke little and when she did her eyes drifted to the broad windows over Palmer's shoulders.

'Mrs Webb, do you know where Matthew is?'

'I always thought he'd be something special,' she told the windows.

'Mrs Webb?'

Her husband was already talking when he entered the room. 'He's overseas, exact whereabouts unknown. AWOL, you could say.'

Palmer noted he was as gruff in real life as he had been on the phone. He was much older than his son. And, for that matter, his wife. His face was a mess of broken veins and his girth exceeded his shirt on several sides.

'Are you worried about him?' Palmer asked.

'We were, when you failed to incarcerate that bloody stalker.'

Palmer looked between the two of them, at the doctor's sneer and his wife's blank gaze. She had a sudden desire to tell them about Mary's prediction. She wanted to see what it would do to their expressions, knowing Matthew was going to be a celebrated researcher.

'Matthew told me you wouldn't let him quit his medical degree. How'd you let him go overseas during exams?'

'Kid needed to get out of the city. After you failed to be of any assistance whatsoever.'

'Does he have a credit card?'

'He's a subsidiary on his mother's.'

'So you'd see his bills?'

'Lord, we don't examine them! He needed a break, we gave him money for a plane ticket. The kid was worn down.'

Funny way to refer to his own son. Distant, like he was delivering a diagnosis.

Palmer rose and moved to a sideboard littered with expensive liquor and even more expensive art. 'Well, I just wanted to check in with him.' She leaned into a pastel piece of abstract art, feeling Webb Senior's gaze on her.

'Thank you. But you've done enough, Detective,' his voice was sour.

Palmer left, crossing the lawn back to the only non-BMW, non-Mercedes vehicle in the street. Hers. Her phone rang. It was Andrews.

'Tim O'Donnell passed away. I'm sorry, Laura.'

Palmer hung up. *The future was now*, she realised. And Contrary Mary's predictions were beginning to turn out right. Tim never had forgiven her.

Palmer was angry. About Tim, about Mary, about the missing Matthew. She was also hungover. Andrews had refused to come home with her, but he had agreed to stay up until dawn, toasting the late Tim O'Donnell.

'For Tim,' he'd say when she got too close. And Palmer would freeze, back off, agree to another drink.

'There's an investigation,' Palmer said. 'I'm not going to come out strictly clean.'

'You can't be sure—'

'She told me. Mary.'

Andrews looked interested. 'She tell you if you'd be cleared?'

Palmer took a swallow of something. She wasn't sure what she was drinking anymore, but it burned in a satisfying way. 'Not quite.'

'As in, she didn't quite tell you? Or you're not quite cleared?'

'The second one, sort of,' Palmer paused to let that sink in. 'I can kiss my police career goodbye. It's wall to wall freak shows and weird cases from here on in. Every goddamn one. I'm cursed.'

'By Tim?'

She hadn't meant that, but maybe it made sense. Maybe Tim was the reason she'd be getting a string of career-ending cases from now on.

'The "cursed" thing was my interpretation. She didn't actually mean Tim's sitting around in the afterlife, cursing people. Well, I don't think so anyhow.'

Andrews sighed, pushed his empty glass around in a puddle of condensation on the bar. 'There's still good work to be done, even on the weird cases. People will always need help. Maybe more so.'

'Whatever,' Palmer swallowed more fire. 'Tell me about Mary. What did she see in her own future? Apart from this whole "bigger picture" thing.'

Andrews refused to tell, at first. But his weakness was scotch, and hers was her need to solve the riddle Mary had left behind. So in the end he told her.

'She said she'd go to pieces.'

Palmer paused. 'That's it?'

So Andrews had shown her what Mel had done next. He mimed cutting a sawing motion across his neck.

'Someone cuts her head off? Jesus,' Palmer grimaced. 'That is fucked up. Beheaded. By who?'

'Whom,' Andrews raised his glass. 'I asked her that.'

'And?'

'She giggled like a schoolgirl. Then she said that thing about a bigger picture.'

He gave Palmer a look she remembered. Or, rather, a look her skin remembered. She ached to her toes.

'Whatever happened to Tim, anyhow?' Andrews said, like he was always ready with a diversion. 'Where were you when he was shot?'

'He had some lead, some crazy idea he'd gotten about a junkie with a racket in stolen gems.'

'A junkie? Unusual.'

'We checked it out,' Palmer shrugged. 'Junkie said he was finding them—get this—behind his ears.'

'Another of your weird cases?'

'So it turned out. But back then, I didn't know it. We went in armed.'

She hesitated.

Andrews said, 'Junkies are unpredictable.'

'Especially this one. He could transform things. I swear my gun was in my holster when I went in. But when I reached for it...'

'It wasn't there?'

'It was diamonds.'

'You going to tell the investigation that?'

She raised her glass, gesturing the barman for another drink. 'How could I?'

She made an excuse to leave and spent the next week ignoring his calls. Every morning she woke up with an image of Mary cutting off her own head. Either as consequence or distraction, she took to staking out Webb Senior. There was something he wasn't telling her and plus, she didn't like him.

Webb was smart, but she didn't think he was observant—a

factor either of age or arrogance. Two weeks later she followed him to a remote part of Sydney Uni campus that looked more like garden than city. He left his car parked across the doorway of a squat white building. Few people passed, student or otherwise. So when Matthew appeared, she spotted him easily.

'I'll be damned,' she threw half a sandwich onto the passenger seat of her car and sat up straighter.

He was smoking, which surprised her, and he had that same edgy look about him he'd had when they met. She recognised that even more than she recognised him. She got out of the car.

'Matthew Webb. How was your trip?'

Matthew started. 'Detective, what're you doing here?'

'Looking for your stalker,' she scanned the perimeter. 'Seen her lately?'

'Um…'

'You remember her, right? I'm talking three, four months ago. She could turn up before you arrived.'

'Yeah. Sure.' He gave a smooth shadow of a smile, something they'd probably taught him at doctor school. 'I guess I haven't seen her. I owe you, Detective. You must have frightened her off. '

'She didn't seem frightened to me.' She changed the subject. 'Had a few chats with your dad these past weeks. He says you're planning a career in cancer after all.'

'Yeah, he mentioned you'd been following him. Said he's started laying a place at the table for you.'

'I'm touched. What should I bring?'

'I wouldn't.' Matthew half-smiled. Beads of sweat lined his brow. 'My mum's a lousy cook.'

'So I'll pack sandwiches. Maybe I'll pack some for you, too, Matthew. You don't look so good.'

'I'm fine. My dad's got me on something.'

'Same stuff your mum's on?' She shook her head. 'I wouldn't.'

'Thanks, Detective. I know you're trying to be helpful.'

'Sure, and I'll keep trying.' She moved suddenly towards the building.

Matthew stiffened, trying to make like he hadn't. He took a step backwards but Palmer was faster. She ducked around him and into the doorway.

Inside was a staircase. She took the stairs two at a time and found herself outside a room with a narrow glass panel in the door. Inside, Matthew's father was dressed in a lab coat and leaning over what looked to be a metal examining table.

'Listen,' said Matthew, catching up to her. 'Detective, can I talk to you?'

Palmer pushed the door open. 'We can talk in here.'

Doctor Webb looked up in surprise. He gave her a sly smile. 'Why, Detective Palmer.'

Palmer sized up the room. Wherever she looked, she saw body parts, cold, clinically carved into anonymous learning tools for medical students. Neat, almost plasticised, but still real parts of real people. The smell was part butcher, part meth lab. She tried not to gag. She tried not to think about Mary's prediction, about Andrews miming a saw across his neck.

'Jesus.' She fixed her gaze on Webb Senior. On the table in front of him was a human torso, the front stripped to the organs inside.

'Ever been in a teaching lab before, Detective?' Doctor Webb smiled. 'It can seem gruesome at first. But cadaver research is a critical tool. As I've been telling Matthew, you have to put your qualms aside. See the bigger picture.'

Palmer was cold. 'Sounds familiar.'

He looked confused. 'Beg pardon?'

'You ever use that phrase to Matthew's stalker?'

'My God. Why would I? I'm not holding discourse with the city's disenfranchised, Detective.'

Palmer swung her gaze to Matthew. He had the clear, watchful gaze of a man about to hang. Like he could live an entire lifetime in whatever minutes he had left if only he kept his eyes open wide enough. 'Is she here, Matthew?'

'Who are you after, Detective?' Webb Senior cut in. 'A lost family member? An old friend? It breaks the rules, but you're welcome to look around. Mind you, we rarely keep the heads. Too personal.'

Palmer remembered Mary, those layers of sweaters and stockings she wore, even in summer. There was nothing she'd recognise about Mary but that flat face and the way she swung her arms.

She turned back to the door. Behind her Doctor Webb chuckled in dry, high-pitched heaves. She continued down and away from the lab, towards the door and a patch of daylight. She glanced up and found Matthew on the landing above, watching her.

'The bigger picture, Matthew? That what you did to her?'

Matthew looked sick. 'I don't know anything about that.'

'Because you don't want to know?' She felt a bitter familiarity. 'I'm betting it was your dad's idea to hide her here. Whatever's left of her. Am I right?'

'I don't know what happened to her! He says she's gone. Maybe he paid her off or—'

'You're smarter than that.'

Matthew didn't answer.

Tim hadn't forgiven her, and she would live with that curse forever. Even now, she wasn't sure what she'd do differently. And now Mary was dead, too. Because Palmer had been too slow.

'Detective, I need help,' Matthew said. He hesitated. 'I … hear things. Voices. I can hear … someone talking to me. All the time. I swear I'm losing my mind, you know?'

She knew. She shifted her weight. 'Someone's stalking you in your head now, Matthew?'

'No, I—'

'Because I'd put that down to a guilty conscience.' She took a business card from her pocket and raised it in the air between them. 'You ever need to talk, you give me a call.'

She laid the card on the stairs. Then turned and left him to his bigger picture.

Web of Lies

The room kept snapping into focus and bleeding out again. The drinks—the *how many?* drinks—made it hard to put one thought in front of another. His head throbbed. Some old man was talking to him, jowls wobbling like turkey combs.

'I'm sorry for your loss,' said the old man.

Wobble for your loss.

'Thanks.'

'I used to work with your father. He was a great man, Matthew.'

'So he said.'

The man started, laughed under his breath so he didn't disrupt the wake, gave Matthew a keen look. Like he understood something. Matthew felt a sudden warmth towards the man, even offered him a drink from the bottle he seemed permanently unable to release from his clenched fist.

His mother appeared, flat out appeared like she'd stepped out of a dark room, *how did she do that?* Black dress buttoned to her collarbone, discreet grey pearls at the base of her throat. She was tall, big-boned in the face, hair swept up in an old-fashioned bun.

'You'll miss him, Mrs Webb,' said the old man, Turkey Combs, 'he-was-a-great-man.'

Matthew's mother made anonymous, consoling noises like she wasn't even listening. Her eyes were fixed on Matthew. The haze of grief-fuelled alcohol made it hard for him to focus but he knew she was watching him because when he swayed he could see her dark eyes follow him. *Portrait*, he thought, *of a freaking lady*. It creeped him the hell out.

'Creepy,' he heard himself say. He giggled.

'Matthew?' his mother sneered or smiled, he wasn't sure.

'I'm okay.' He waved the bottle in his fist as some kind of proof.

There was something not-right about her today. It wasn't that she hadn't cried, that was the most normal thing about this whole day. Matthew had known her twenty-three years and never seen her cry. She'd spent the last couple of decades in a chemical envelope that seemed not just to minimise emotions but to eliminate them entirely. That's when he got it. She was sober. Now, *that* was creepy.

'I'll miss him,' Matthew said. Out loud, apparently, because Turkey Combs slapped him on the shoulder.

'Of course you will, son.'

Son. Not even his dad had ever called him that.

'I feel bad.' Matthew staggered.

His mother caught him by the elbow and steered him to the front door. He sagged against her, taking in the smell of her perfume and the feel of her iron grip on his arm. He was glad for the support. Until she took his glass.

'Hey,' he said, but couldn't work out a follow-up.

'Don't let your father ruin you.'

'Whoa, Mum? Wow. He just *died*, for chrissake.'

She tipped the empty glass in a kind of salute. 'My point, exactly.' Close up he saw there was a wisp of grey hair tucked behind her ear, a single pearl earring sagging on her soft lobe. When had her hair gone grey, anyhow? 'How about you go sleep it off, Matthew. People will talk.'

'That's the problem,' Matthew slurred, straightened, tried to keep his words in order. 'That's the problem. They never stop talking.'

'What are you saying?'

'I hear things.'

'Is that what it is?' She gave him a look like he was a puzzle she'd only just worked out. 'Is that why your father kept you drugged?'

She hadn't seemed that interested in anything he'd said in years. Maybe, ever. 'Is that why he kept *you* drugged?'

She rolled her eyes. 'Oh, well done, Matthew. Marvellous comeback.'

'Sorry, Mum, sorry. Are you feeling okay?'

Twin points of cold light in her pupils. She said, 'Why on earth would I be feeling okay?'

She took his bottle from his slack fist and shoved him out the door.

***

Guilt, the cop had called it, but that wasn't right. No, it was something worse. He slouched in the driver's seat, pulled a bottle of bourbon out from under it to wash down a benzodiazepine. He watched the house and thought about his mother, dry-faced at the wake, upright at the funeral. A hook of a woman with a bend to her spine she'd hate to acknowledge. Usually so sunk in medical euphoria her pupils floated like buoys.

She was right, though. His father had kept him prescribed, kept him insulated from the voices in his head. His father was gone for good now, he realised with a sharp dread in his gut. For good or for bad. What was he going to do now, him and his weirdly sober, creepy mother? They'd lost their source. He was struck by a sudden familial emotion which he figured was more duty than care. Maybe she was just out of her prescription. Maybe he could help her out. Or maybe he would hoard the remainder of his pills for as long as he could. If he ever graduated he could prescribe his own damn medicinal buffer.

'I'll drink to that,' he said out loud and raised the bourbon for another swig.

'Are you seeing the bigger picture yet, my boy?'

He jumped. His father's voice, unbidden in his head. He knew he was alone, knew his father was dead. But that didn't stop him taking a quick look around the car interior, at the empty seats behind him and even the dirty footwells. Nothing. Of course, nothing. He was going crazy.

'Sure, Dad. Bigger picture. Cheers.' He toasted the old man. The bourbon burned in an immediate way that took his mind off what was to come. Whatever that was. 'Been a long time,' he crooned, forgetting the rest of the words. Then wondered if it had ever been a song at all. 'Ah, hell.'

It had been a long time since he'd tried to live in direct relation to the world. Which was to say, without a prescription. He didn't think he was ready. Outside the car, everything seemed to throb. The house ballooned and the driveway twisted and the sky rolled like so much oil on water. He shut his eyes and fell into something more hollow than sleep. Strange things called to him by name and refused to show their faces.

When he woke it was dark, but not night. A summer storm had thickened the grey clouds overhead. With his father's illness-death-funeral, much of a year had passed him by. He checked his watch. Three in the afternoon. The house was quiet. The wake must be over. He thought about his mother, alone in the empty house with her grief. That iron mountain of a woman. He started the car and backed out of the driveway.

On the road he drove almost randomly, unsure where to go. Life had become an interim thing. A reaction, a quick-fix while he worked out what-to-do-next. Problem was, what to do next was always one more half-step in an ill-thought-out and random direction. Never anything sustainable, never really getting hold of—

'The bigger picture.'

'Oh, shut up,' Matthew muttered.

A skull-buzzing migraine bloomed behind his eyes, only partly a hangover. He thumbed the benzo bottle and tipped a couple into his mouth, rolling them around until he could get them under his tongue. Bitterness flooded his mouth, but he'd long associated bitterness with salvation. He shook the bottle. Nothing more rattled inside.

'Goddammitt.'

He should go home, get a fresh supply. But first he'd go visit the lab. It was on the way or sort of. One of the last places he'd seen his dad and he felt the need to honour his old man. Not that Matthew was sentimental. His father used to crow that they'd bred sentimentality out of the Webbs three generations of surgeons ago.

'I ain't sentimental,' he crooned.

The Harbour Bridge was as iron grey as the sky. The ocean stretched flat and pale either side. Most cars had their lights on to combat the cloud cover. Matthew should probably do the same, but superstitiously he didn't want to draw attention to himself. He was too wiped to work out how well he was driving, but he didn't want to jinx himself. The lights stayed off.

'The perfection of practice, hey, Dad?'

Another one of his dad's phrases. *Or maybe it was the practice of perfection? Whatever.* Truth was, Matthew wasn't what you'd call a natural at medicine, and no amount of cajoling from his father had changed that. He remembered that no-son-of-mine look in the old man's eyes when his dad had worked that out. Matthew Webb, fourth generation doctor. And lousy at it.

'Practice is perfection, perfection is practice,' his dad's voice again.

'Thanks, Dad.'

'Not that I needed the practice. I was gifted.'

'You're a natural, Dad.'

'Don't take that tone with me.'

Matthew froze. His car kept moving though and at the last minute he had to brake hard. He was in Chinatown and the traffic was slow. He should be paying more attention. 'Dad?'

No answer.

'Dad, are you ... *actually* talking to me?'

Still nothing. Of course, nothing, what did he expect? That the old man was really talking to him? Beyond the freaking *grave*? Crazy. Stupid. Absurd, to use one of his mother's words. But then, the voices he used to hear, before the prescriptions, they'd seemed real, too. Nonsense his father had told him, and Matthew had agreed. He'd scored a hefty dose of anti-psychotics for his agreement, so it seemed like the right thing to do.

'Crazy, Dad. Crazy.'

He waited, glancing left and right. No one answered.

When he reached the lab it was open, the smell of phenol and formalin so thick in the corridor he felt he could almost grab fistfuls of the stuff from the air. The door was open but the lab itself looked empty. Which was to say, empty of anything living. This was an anatomy lab. Banks of metal drawers four feet high were pushed against every wall, and in every drawer was a human cadaver. The relentless white noise of the ventilation system sounded spookily like a distant roar of conversation. Entering the room felt like crossing a threshold between the living and the dead.

'Matty Webb. Come for some extra-curricular?'

Matthew jumped and spun in a half-crouch. Which startled the heck out of the (living, not dead) tutor who'd followed him into the room. The guy raised his arms defensively while Matthew struggled to remember his name. Maybe Wayne, maybe Warren. He stuck with Wayne, waved a hand in greeting and eased out of the crouch he'd been in.

'Uh, sure.' He'd never been called Matty before. He wasn't sure he liked it.

'I'll help,' Wayne gestured with a set of lab tongs. 'Cultures are cooking and I'm bored out of my mind with the waiting.'

Matthew said, 'Great,' but didn't mean it.

Wayne was tall, lean, with dark red hair tied back in a ponytail to his shoulders and then some. He had a black goatee and incongruous red stubble. He wore cowboy boots and a plaid shirt, and jeans that could probably stand upright on their own.

'Where do we start, dude?' Wayne asked.

Dude. Somewhere in Wayne's head it was still the Eighties.

'How about … anywhere. Dude.'

Wayne snapped his tongs and gave Matthew a thoughtful look. Then he moved to a bank of deep stainless steel drawers, six drawers in two rows of three. He slid out a metal tray and pulled back a soft off-white cloth, exposing beneath its load of human flesh: the neatly arranged corpse of a man as indifferent as plasticine, skin removed to reveal a gristle of muscle and congealed organs in the deep, garish colours of bruising.

'So, young Doctor Webb, tell me. What killed this gentleman?'

If Matthew struggled with most of his medical studies, where he really flunked was diagnostics. 'Heart attack?'

'Oh, man. You're not even trying.'

Matthew leaned in for a closer look. Why not? It was a good distraction.

A body had to last years in an anatomy lab. Not many people left their bodies to science, so specimens were most often sourced from people with no homes or names, and no one to claim their bodies when they died.

'Practice is perfection,' came his father's voice again.

Matthew jumped. Wayne jumped, too, and he gave Matthew a startled look.

'Did you hear that?' Matthew asked.

'Hear what?'

'That voice, "practice is perfection". My dad's voice.'

Wayne looked uncomfortable. 'What, you expecting your dad here today?'

'No,' said Matthew. 'I'm really not.'

'Good, 'cos your dad is kinda scary. He flunked me right as I was gonna graduate. Made me repeat a year.'

'And then told you to keep practising?' Wayne gave him a grateful look, which Matthew tried to ignore. He turned away, back to the drawer.

'Uhhh…' He had no idea what had killed this guy. He should go home.

His father's voice returned. 'Near the intestine, lower right.'

'What, the appendix?'

Wayne raised an eyebrow. 'Found something, little doctor buddy?'

The body stank of fixatives so bad Matthew could taste it. He leaned to one side, peering under the grey flab of intestine. The appendix should have looked like a narrow tube lightly pink, but this one was fat and bulbous and, even post-mortem, a deep dark red.

'It's ruptured,' Matthew said.

'Great work, dude. Maybe you have been practising. Another?' Wayne closed the drawer and opened the one below.

Matthew squatted, hands hanging limply between his knees. He felt light-headed and scared. Mainly scared. More scared than usual, and he'd been scared for years. Since the voices began. A superstitious dread prickled his scalp as he looked at the corpse. It was a woman's body. He could tell from the distinction between hips and waist, since the breasts had been cut away in a partial dissection. She'd been old, judging by her skin and the white of her pubic hair, still visible under the pocket of exposed organs.

His father's voice was clear. 'You'll love this one.'

'Ah, man, too weird,' Matthew muttered.

'You wanna take a break, buddy?'

'Nah, I got nowhere to be. Um, let me think,' he paused, praying for his father's voice. 'Her lungs are pretty yellow?'

'Smoker,' his father said dismissively. 'That's not what killed her.'

Matthew started. 'You didn't hear that either, right?'

'Dude, should you be on something?' Wayne cocked his head.

Matthew reflected that, yeah, he should. The buzzing in his head was getting worse. Like an ocean in his skull, waves of noise crashing against the sides. No, more like static. Like a hundred untuned radio stations all at once. He needed another benzo. He reached for his pocket, but remembered the empty bottle. Wayne gazed at him curiously and Matthew gave him a weak smile.

Come on, Dad.

The buzzing really was resolving into voices, but not his father's this time. One voice stood out, crackling with age. She described something that felt like walking on hot coals, the soles of her feet scorching.

'Burns?' Matthew leaned around to check her feet. Nothing. Okay, not burns.

Wayne gave him a strange look. 'That was totally random.'

The voice was stronger. She described numbness, blurred vision, prickling in her fingertips, breath growing heavy.

'Poison?' Matthew said. He caught Wayne's gaze. 'I mean…'

He didn't need a medical degree to know the symptoms of poison, just a few episodes of *CSI*. And those were poison symptoms.

'Don't talk to this fool about murder, he might begin to suspect something,' his father muttered.

'Oh, geez. I mean.' *Shit*. 'I'm not sure. What killed her, that is.'

Wayne sighed. 'You had some far out guesses, buddy. Says here plain old heart disease.' He held up the toe-tag.

'Of course it does.' His father's voice. 'I wrote it.'

'You really are talking to me.'

Wayne frowned. 'Well, of course I am.'

'I had to hide her somewhere.'

'Oh, God.'

'You should sit down, dude. You look like hell.'

'I just need my pills, Wayne, for chrissake.'

'Wayne? Dude, that's not my name.'

'Whatever.' Matthew lurched to his feet and reeled out of the room.

His stomach lurched. In the corridor he retched against a wall. Yellow bile draped from his lips in a stringy curtain, clinging to his chin.

A familiar chuckle began in his skull, an old woman's chuckle with an edge of madness. A woman who used to stalk him, who'd turn up at his lectures, his home, his bus stop, a woman who always seemed to know right where he'd be before he did.

The woman said. 'Hey, boy. Ask me where you'll be in fifty years.'

'Jesus.'

The skull-buzz threatened to overwhelm him, throbbing into his temples like it was bent on escaping through the bone. He pressed his temple to the wall. A sharp blackness echoed up his nose. His skin burned. Panic prickled along his chest and neck. He catalogued the symptoms of withdrawal, repeating them like a mantra.

'Dude, are you having an episode?' Not-Wayne asked.

'I need my pills.'

'What pills are you on?' Wayne asked. 'I could maybe write you a prescription. There's a chemist—'

'Can you do me some Clorazepate?'

'Whoa,' Wayne reeled back, 'why are you on anxiolytics?'

'Can you help me or not?'

Wayne hesitated. 'I'm not comfortable with that. Maybe you need a psychiatrist. Hey, wait. Matty, where you going?'

He was sure of it now. He hated to be called Matty.

He backtracked along the corridor and fled outside to his car. Sometimes there was a spare bottle in the glove box. Maybe today was one of those days. Maybe before the funeral he'd stashed a bottle in the glove box for later. That was one of the fun facts of brain-altering substances, you were never sure what you'd already done. It was like having a housemate you never saw.

Nothing in the glove box. He leaned into the footwells, passing his hand back and forth across worn carpet, head pounding until he vomited up funeral booze all over his front tyre. He sat on the ground, alternating between swearing and praying, sweat dripping from his face. He couldn't hear any of his own words over the voices crowding his head.

That's what his father had been protecting him from. The weird cacophony of voices that took hold. His arms ached, pins and needles spread across his fingertips and toes. Maybe his mother had a stash she'd be willing to share. He dialled her number.

'Mum, I need a prescription—'

He heard the sound of something rattling down the phone line. Like pills in a plastic vial.

'Matthew, we're going cold turkey, you and I.'

'Wait. Mum. What you do, that's up to you. But I need my pills.'

'You only think you do.'

'No. Dad understood—'

'That's hard to believe. Your father, understanding something. Let's see what you *need* when your father's not around to control you.'

'Mum! This isn't just in my head.'

'I'm coming to your house,' she told him. 'For the rest of the pills.'

She was crazy. She had no idea what he was going through. He tried to explain, shouting into the phone until he realised she'd hung up. He checked his watch. Not yet five. If he could make it home, get to the prescription before she did, there was time to find a chemist.

The drive was hard, voices pounding his ears, booming in his eye sockets. A valley of grey grit hung in front of his nose. He couldn't blink it away and he was pretty sure it was shearing his skull apart. His hands were clammy on the steering wheel. His leg jittered on the foot pedals, rocking the car. He took the corner to his street at a wide swerve and the car fishtailed once before righting itself.

His father said, 'Steady, Matthew. You're on the cusp of something great. Don't throw it away.'

'You've been talking to me this whole time.'

'Of course. You think you solved that ruptured appendix on your own?'

'But then *she* started talking to me. That woman you murdered, you freaking—' He didn't have words for what his dad was.

'Imagine it, son, with my brains and your talent for hearing the dead—' Matthew was out of the car and staggering towards his house, trying to run. As if he could run away from his father's voice. But everywhere he went, it followed.

He scanned the street. No sign of his mother's car.

'You'll be a star, my boy. You hear their symptoms, I diagnose them.'

'I don't want to be a star, Dad. I want to be normal.'

'No sane person ever wanted that, son,' his father scoffed.

He cursed the old man. Dead, he was more present than ever. Matthew ran up a flight of stairs and let himself into his apartment with shaking hands. His mother was already there. She'd changed into a soft tracksuit, drawstrings hanging from her shoulders. Her eyes were pink all the way through to her pupils and her face was pinched. It had her, he realised. The withdrawal.

She stood beside the filing cabinet, an empty pill vial in one hand, and in the other his last two prescriptions.

'Mum?'

She smiled. She looked almost sorry for him.

'Your father had many skills,' she began, 'but one in particular. He could … *imagine* just the right incision, the

69

right flick of the scalpel, and it would happen. Like magic. I envied him, Matthew. He had such a power.'

'That's great, Mum. I'm glad you shared. Now. Please. Give me the prescriptions.'

She ignored him. 'That's how he was still practising after most of his colleagues retired. Including that idiot at the wake. Did you catch his name?'

'Can't say I did.'

'The hospital kept testing him, of course. Your father. His hands shook like an old man's. But his precision was flawless. Nobody could understand it. It was inexplicable. A miracle, according to your father. Can you believe that? A miracle wasted on someone so … well, how would you describe your father, Matthew?'

'A great man?' Matthew tried fiercely to understand what she was talking about.

'Oh, please. Don't insult my intelligence.'

'Okay.' He raised his hands. 'Okay. He was … talented?'

'He was a fraud,' she corrected him. 'But a successful one. That's what the power can do.'

'What power?'

'Whatever power you have.'

'Mum. It's been a hard day.'

'Get used to it.'

He'd never been able to bargain with her. He tried to come up with another option. He could maybe wrestle her for them, but the thought of touching her—a hard woman in too-soft skin—repulsed him.

'I hear things, Mum. Voices. People talking to me, except

they're dead. It's … a power, I guess. Like Dad's.' He wasn't sure what he expected from her. Surprise, fear. Contempt, most likely. Maybe even pride. But she looked at him with a cold, blank gaze. She seemed almost to relax.

'That homeless woman, she said you'd have something. Some path to fortune and fame. But she wasn't sure what it was. Or, she wasn't sure how to describe it.'

'She told you that? When?'

'Three years ago. She showed up at the house. Said she had something important for me. She knew your name.'

'She was stalking me.'

'She talked about you for a long time, what you'd be, what you'd do. I couldn't remember all of it. So she told me again and made me write it down. She sat with me so long the valium started to wear off and I began to understand. She was telling me you'd be special. Finally. I'd given up. And she told me I'd help you.'

'You've never told me any of this.'

'No. I had to wait for you to realise it yourself. That you can do something no one else can.'

'You want to help me?' Matthew spied an opening. 'How about you hand me those prescriptions.'

'Don't patronise me, Matthew. I had enough of that with your father.'

She moved away from him, turning her back. He thought about hitting her but there was nothing to hand.

'I chose him for his talent, you know. Your father. He was the only man I knew who had any kind of power. And I wanted children with power, too. Like me.'

'You wanted children?'

She smirked, turning back casually. 'Yes, it surprises me, too, looking back on it. But once upon a time I wanted a dozen children. I also wanted a life, but apparently I couldn't have both. Not according to your father.'

'You gave up a career. To be with Dad, isn't that right?'

'A very promising career, yes. To be with your father. To raise our children. Well, our child, as it turned out.'

Matthew's mind was racing, seeking another out. His mother watched him with a predatory keenness.

'I thought your talent would be obvious, you see. From birth. I watched you and I *watched* you. But you were an ordinary baby.'

'Sorry I disappointed you, Mum.'

'And I was disappointed. Until that homeless woman filled me in. What was her name?'

Matthew shook his head. 'I don't know.'

'Really? She changed all our lives, and you don't even know her name? That's a shame.'

Yeah, it was a real shame. Matthew rushed at her, hoping to overpower her. She reached out a hand like she was going to pat his face, but at the last moment her fist clenched. Such a delicate fist, skin smoothed by all the best moisturisers money could buy, blue veins standing out underneath. Matthew tried to speak but what came out was a gasp. A sharp pain scissored through his chest, exploding into his shoulder and arm. His vision went red and he could hear himself choking. He fell to one knee.

'You were a sickly child,' she murmured, 'so everyone thought. Your dad told me it was a blessing I had my own medical education. A blessing. I agreed, but not for the reasons he thought. I knew just which organs to squeeze, and for how long, and what the pain would be. What your father didn't quite get was that you weren't the sickly one. I suppose I was.' She regarded him with cool detachment.

He'd grown up with that look. It was familiar and so was the pain. Years of pain and inexplicable illnesses. A dozen diagnoses. Ulcers, fibromyalgia, even gastric cancer. They hadn't diagnosed his mother with anything at all as she stood bravely by his bedside, fists clenched in fear for her little boy.

'Mum, why?'

She relaxed her hand and the pain lifted. She sized him up with a fierce curiosity. Matthew slumped to the ground, gasping. 'I was a talented student, Matthew. I could have been a talented doctor. But I stupidly chose to marry someone who didn't want the competition.'

'I was a kid, for chrissake.'

She raised her hand and he winced and reached up, snagging her wrist. 'Don't.'

'I killed her.'

'What?'

'You didn't ask, but I thought you should know. I killed that woman who was stalking you.'

Matthew hesitated. 'I thought Dad did it.'

'He didn't have the initiative for a job like that. I called him up when it was done. He took care of the body.'

'Wow, that's cold.'

She drew thumb and forefinger together and Matthew collapsed to the floor, retching and gagging. When the pain passed he slouched against the couch, gasping. His heart pounded and he was having trouble getting air into his lungs.

He took a breath, tried to steady himself, 'Did you kill Dad, too?'

His mother smiled that slow smile. Her voice, when she spoke, was calm. 'You don't choose your power, Matthew. It chooses you. I could have been granted the power to heal, but I wasn't. There's few uses for a power like mine. Few good uses. But I found one. I used it to get someone's attention.'

'Dad's?'

'No,' she laughed in that head-thrown-back way he'd never even imagined she could do.

'The man from the Grey Institute. Esser Grey.'

'That guy? He's in prison.'

'Hasn't stopped him. He's going to pay us to work with him.'

'To do what?'

'Whatever our talents dictate we should do. He says we all have a reason.'

'The Grey Institute—is it a lab?' Matthew saw the anatomy lab again, those metal drawers of meat. He wondered what a lab would do to him, and whether he cared anymore. Anything that would silence the voices in his head.

'Better,' said his mother. 'It's a beginning.'

Bad Power

I had me listed as a bad man. Seemed the best way to hide. Especially true for a woman, it was that or run. Lord knows I was tired of running, I been running all my life. 'Cos the world ain't safe for women and the world ain't safe for me, whatever I am.

I says, 'I look like a man, right?'

'Sure, some,' says Chella.

He preferred men, so that was a compliment.

'You gonna hid in plain sight nows?' he asks, and when I confirmed it he says, 'You tired of the road, tired of running, then you tired of living and every place but death.'

He was right, often he was. Chella was running just 'cos he liked it. Had nothing better to do and no past but a string of crimes didn't want to own up to. He planned to go out like a fighter. I figured his future didn't hold that, but I never knew how to tell him. He didn't live like a fighter, sure couldn't see him dying like one.

'Never met one like you,' he'd say often, half-impressed and half-otherwise. Looking at me with that superstition

I came to take as normal for everyone who weren't me or blood to me.

Looking back nows, I think Chella never liked me. He just couldn't be away from me. It was a compulsion, him to me. Me to him also, we had that in common. Sometimes he'd follow and sometimes he'd lead and so we rolled around each other like spokes in a wheel. When he'd up and want to leave I'd tell him, 'Don't go,' and that'd be it. He'd stay. And when I wanted to go … well, I never did. Chella scared me like that. Had a power over me I didn't right understand, made me want no one but him. Goddamn him for that.

I thought his power would be done when he was dead, but I was wrong. Every man after that was or wasn't Chella. Every woman, too, in her own way. There was nothing remarkable about Chella, you understand, but he had marked me and I had let him and after that, maybe we both of us regretted it.

Chella got sick day by day and the doc—if there was a doc in whatever town we lighted on—the doc would try all sorts of remedies. Potions, salves, balms, all kinds of stink. Leeches one time. Snakes the next, and that was the worst. Half-crazed with voices of his own, that doc. He wasn't all there, but he sure was someplace. To his own mind, at least. Thought himself something. Chella, I think, related to him for that. Chella been driven half-mad by voices when he was just a kid, so he said.

He asks, 'What god you think you're serving, crazy man? What voice you hear?'

Doc says back, 'I serves that there bad man that travels with you and pays my bills. I do his bidding when his voice is in my head. You hear it?'

The doc meant me. He gave me a wink like we knew each other, made my skin crawl. Chella went into a rage, protecting me. He slapped the doc with his good arm 'til the other man howled. But still the doc wouldn't stop winking at me, wanting something from me.

I says to the doc, 'You say you serve me. Well, get lost.'

He took right off, simple as that. Didn't even stop for his purse.

Chella laughed and shook his head at me and I told him to go to hell. He assured me he was already there. The pain, see, from whatever he had. Lifted himself off the doc's cot and eased up onto legs that wobbled under him like saplings holding up a ceiling.

After that, Chella stuck to the docs who offered remedies you could keep in jars. Tried a dozen or so. No match for what he had. Wasted away under his hat, wasted within his clothes, wasted day by day sitting upright, wasting night by night lying on the ground.

'Ah, geez, to hell with this.' He dropped where he walked.

I dragged him off the path and up beside a fallen tree. Pushed aside the scraggling undergrowth, made enemies of a snake was resting there. Snake made good eating once I got it blackened over a fire, but that fire took half a day to light. Then got drowned by rain, and so did we. Rained day and night. Tree trunk kept the worst of it off Chella's face but it pooled under his head and turned the black soil there to bile. I kept wiping it off my clothes until my hands were so covered I was just spreading it around. Then I waited it out.

His last words were *Don't go telling*.

I didn't know which he meant. Don't go telling how he lived or how he died? 'Cos dying is what he did next, he couldn't help it. I felt powerless, but really I was just stubborn. Didn't say nothing that might help him live, but I stayed right by him until his skin was mottled brown and blue and insects crawled over his eyeballs. It felt wrong, to look at bugs on a man's face and not do anything. Worse when he does nothing himself. There we were, on some dirt road, him dead and me wishing I was. I never raised a hand to hurt Chella, that's important. I maybe told him one time that if he was gonna keep complaining about me, or to me, he might as well just go ahead and die. After that he got sick and I was too ashamed to correct myself. Anyhow, I meant nothing by it.

Nothing Chella had was much use to me. His clothes were too big and his boots too old. I took his hat, though. When I ran into family of his out west they recognised it. *Custom-made band*, Chella had told me. Didn't say his sister had made it, didn't say she'd recognise it when I ran into her on the street in the next town that came my way. I guess that's why Chella ended up choosing this road. Maybe he was wanting home. Sickness and death do that, make you choose something you usually wouldn't. Like, family. Your past. Something recognisable in a world that's come out too flat and wide.

So there I was deep in the bosom of Chella's family. More siblings than I had fingers. Father dead, mother on the way. A queue of graves out back, some of them small. I asks, 'Children?'

Chella's brother says, 'Sure, some.'

'Any of 'em Chella's?'

'Reckon.'

Not big talkers, the family, I liked that about them. But I had no place there and when Chella's sister started making eyes at me, I figured it was time to get out. Wasn't nothing wrong with her, just that she took me for a bad man. And also she wasn't my type, for all she reminded me of Chella. She wasn't him.

Brother saw me leaving, 'Chella always did enjoy the company of bad types. What's your name, sir?'

'Does it matter?'

He grunted at that. Told me he wanted a name for the memory. I said to call me Bad and he did, right there and then. He looked like he meant it, too.

***

Next town I fell into I found me a crowd. Town had no name and neither did the men I met. Names ain't much. Can't trade 'em or sell 'em or use 'em for soap. Chella would've been mad. He had the skill of avoiding the darkness in a man. I didn't, though. Probably why me and him ended up together. Neither of us ready for what the other was.

This one man in the crowd, he had a knowing in him.

'You got a power,' he says to me.

'No power I got, not now, not ever. Else I'd be some other place,' I tells him. 'Better places to be than here.'

He laughs. 'You got a power over men, I'd wager.'

He was too specific, and I was wrong. I did have a power. I just didn't know it.

He talked to me in a thick, dark voice I didn't right like. I seen lust on a man and it only ever looked good on Chella. When this man grabbed for me I yelled so loud others came running, looking for a fire. This man shoved me quick, out of the way and into a rail.

'Don't you mind his yelling,' says the man. 'Little bad man's just seen a snake.'

Rest of them laughed and spat and laughed some more while my face burned. My spine had a throb in it from being pushed against the railing. I was holding my shirt closed where he'd torn at me.

I spat to clear the juice in my throat. 'I got a power, huh? I got a power, well get away from me. How about that? Y'all get the hell away from me.'

They was all laughing, but each one took a handful of steps back, laughing but looking kinda worried, too. Like they was confused by what they was doing. Guess he was right, that man. He had an insight and I had a power. First of my kind, too, no one ever had a power like mine. Didn't realise what I had, and how could I? Nothing to compare it to. Nothing like me in history. Halla-freaking-luyeah.

The men all left me alone after that. Wouldn't come any place near me, though in the dark I inched towards their fire so I could warm my hands. I heard them speaking in whispers, probably about me, but any that caught sight of me backed off into the dark and wouldn't look me in the eye. Soon enough I was the only one at that fire. Seemed a shame to waste it. I lay flat and slept, first time in a long time. Soaking up the warmth and stoking the flames when the cold woke me.

First light I rolled up my blanket and stood, picked up Chella's hat and stuck it on my head.

'See you, bad man,' one man says from where he sat hunched into his fellows, shivering in the frost where the fire didn't reach.

'No, you won't be seeing me no more.'

'Thank the devil.'

When I passed, he winced and hunkered down. I thought at the time, maybe that's my power. Maybe I make men afraid. But I just hadn't worked it out yet, what my power was. Turns out that's not a power. That's a consequence.

A lot of people, they never seen the list of bad men. But when I says my name is on it, they believe. Something about my eyes, most of them say. Something about the way I hold myself. One place, though, law men stopped me and made to check. They says my chin or my throat or my something. Made them think twice about me being any kinda man at all. They was pretty direct. Reached for what was between my legs.

I saw those toughened fingers come at me. 'Don't you touch me, law man.'

And the hands of this man, they halted right in mid-air, with me looking at him funny and him looking at his hands funny. He was a big man, too. Shoulders thicker than his skull, buttons straining on his shirt. Think he'd trade a shirt in once it got too small, but probably found some status in a collar and buttons, couldn't afford to trade up.

Other law man was further away. Saw his friend stop still and he made to come over.

'What's with you, Fred?' him shouting.

I tells him to back in hell off. And he did, just like I says. Backed off so fast he tripped over his heels and fell and just kept crawling away on his cheeks. He looked like he'd seen the devil or found gold or both.

Old man by a drinking trough, beard so long it passed the string holding up his trousers, he was watching and laughing. Looking at these two officers of the law turned to mud. When I looked to him he held up hands like he was surrendering. 'Don't do it, crazy lady, don't go using your powers on me!'

I froze cold. Stupid to think, I hadn't known until then what it was I had. I didn't have looks or smarts, but Chella had never left me, and then I knew why. Because I told him not to. But until that old man put it in words, I didn't think it was power. I was the first with a true power, something that ran its own course apart from biology, that was like some kinda visitation from a demon. I was the first I ever heard of had a power like that or, if I wasn't, then the world sure had a good way of hiding the rest.

In the midst of that catastrophe, all I could think of was

Chella, me telling him to drop dead and him doing it. Took him days, but he did what he was told with a thoroughness that belied his wayward nature. He stuck to dying like he had no choice not to. I hated myself then, not for the first time, but fully. And forever.

Only when I worked through all that in my mind did I realise the other thing the old man had said. Called me a lady. Some people, they got the knowing. Usually they got sympathy, too, seen enough of the world and the human soul to understand the why behind a disguise.

'You keep quiet,' I tells him, and he does. But too late. Others come on.

Every kid growing to adult wants a power. Too stupid to want otherwise. Like happiness, contentment, warm bed and full belly. Think power'll get 'em all that and some. But we should be learned, easier to want too much than what's good for you. Harder to want less. But smarter. Wish I'd learned that sooner. Wish I'd had parents to teach me, not the kinda people what raised me to be no better than them. I should stop wishing. Stupid as wanting.

I got me a real life power over people. But I only got that power one at a time. Can't do two people at once, can't do a crowd. And a crowd's what gathered then, strangers with wet eyes. They circled and I turned within them and we all just kept at it for a time. They outgrew it before I did, began to shift in towards me.

'Back off,' I says to one woman, and she does. Backing straight into the people behind her and carrying them with her. Until they flowed around and filled the gap.

'You, put your hand down. You, walk away far as your legs will take you.'

One man turned, knees pumping. He passed the woman who was still backing away, though she kept pace with him for a time. I tells the same to the others that come, still one by one, still not understanding what I can and can't do. Against their wills they obey me, faces dumb with furious wonder. But for every one that left, another joined the crowd. That's when I got it. The ones walking away, they was telling everyone they passed. They was spreading the word as far as they could travel. I done something stupid with that.

'Cover its mouth.' A man grinning like it's no big deal. My life and death just a thing to him.

'Don't you do that!'

When they came at me all and all, I was powerless. Some, they gagged me with a stinking piece of horse blanket, made me retch until darkness came, thumping into the back of my skull in time with the laughter of that old man by the drinking trough.

I moved in a dark place where the dead and the living spoke to each other. I couldn't tell which I was, so I got to asking. One man, called himself Webb, tells me if he can hear me, well, I must be dead. Even apologises to me like it was a bad thing. Had this manner about him, matter-of-fact like he was just doing his job. I tells him not to apologise, best news I've had in forever. He says the dead, they talk to him and he can't control it.

I pitied him, so I tells him dead is better than haunted. He says that gives him something to look forward to, at least, but he chuckles and tells me there's more work to be done yet. He ain't ready to die, is what I understand from him. So I says to him, 'What if I'm not ready to die yet, either? I got something I should see to.'

'I don't honestly know,' says Webb. 'Perhaps just try to live. See how it goes. Good talking to you.'

I thank him. Something in what he said gave me comfort. Maybe just the knowing I ain't ended yet.

Before I know it, light came rolling in like water round a sink hole and I began to see again. I was laying flat, hard edges of something digging into my sides. A cot, a wooden frame with no stuffing. I shifted out of reach of the edge and guessed Webb was right. Trying to live is sometimes enough.

'Don't try anything,' comes a deep drawl.

I moved my eyes without moving my head, since my head hurt all over. Wasn't no place of it didn't.

A fat man, only way to tell it. A fat man leaning back, I guess on a chair though I couldn't see it. I moved my jaw, testing it out.

'One of us is in prison,' I tells him.

When I talked it sounded like I was chewing through gravel.

'Both of us, as it happens. I'm Sheriff Faden.'

'Yeah? What'd you do, Sheriff, land you in here with me?'

He had a full dirty beard and small eyes like a rat, high on the sides of his head. He brought one arm over his scalp, crooked so his elbow was upright and his hand fell over his ear.

'I was the fool put on this badge.' He thumbed it. The badge was dull and dirty like the rest of him.

'They lock you up for that? This place has a temper.'

'You only just now working that out?'

I rolled my head back to ease the pain in my neck. It didn't help none. All the skin left on me itched. Enough it competed with the ache in every bone. I raised an arm. I was marked in scratches, bruises and blood from fingernail to elbow. My clothes were gone, ripped right through, but I was so covered in mud and blood I didn't feel naked. My right thigh stung hard like it was burned. And then I recognised the stink of cooked skin. 'They branded me?'

Faden stretched, 'And then locked me in here with you, and they didn't give me no key.'

I tongued my teeth one by one, counting what was left. 'So there's no way I can tell you to unlock that door?'

'You can tell me. I just can't do it.'

'And if I tell you to take your chair and smash in that window?' I raised a hand, but it was random. My arms were so beat up they moved of their own accord, and my fingers stuck together with blood enough I couldn't point far enough to even pick my own nose.

'That one over there, with the bars?' Faden pointed, more successfully. 'Or that other one, also with bars?'

I didn't answer for a time. I was chewing through my options. 'I could make you beat that chair over your own head 'til you died.'

'Reckon you could.' He shifted on his invisible chair. 'Of course, you'd be alone in here, no one to talk to, no one to boss about. But that might suit you, who's to judge?'

I probably shouldn't have blamed him, but I did. I pictured him with a bullet hole messing up his forehead. Way he told it, he'd done me a favour. He knew if he let me out I'd be for slaughter. Plenty of people hated me. Some, apparently, were still trying to fetch back the people I'd sent away. Faden laughed when he told it, said nothing was stopping those people backing away or walking. Wearing their feet to stumps. Faden didn't care much for the human race, I figured. Guess we had that in common.

'They're planning to kill you piece by piece,' him breathing heavy through his nose, running out of laughter. He frowned, waiting for me to say something but I was pretty much out of words by then. 'That bother you?'

'Bother you?' I asks. 'Ain't you the law?'

'For want of a better occupation.'

We fell quiet, him fat and heavy in his chair, me finding ways to nurse the bruises on my hips or settle the ache in my spine one by one. No way to do both at one time.

'Bothers me,' I admits at last. 'Not for my own self. But for the baby.'

'The what?' Way he says it, dumb and slow, made me hate him more. He stirred in his chair, hands coming down to grab each other in his lap. He figured I was lying. But this was one time I was telling the truth. This was the one thing I'd come back for, from the darkness. To see my child right.

'You heard me, I reckon.'

'This some trick?' Still insisting I was making it up. 'Why'd you be on the road in your condition?'

I almost laughed. Road takes anyone, doesn't discriminate. Mothers, fathers and children. Takes 'em and often doesn't ever let 'em go. I wondered if Chella would've ever stopped running. Maybe if he'd known about our child. Maybe not.

'Figured I could out-run it, I guess. But turns out pregnant is something you can't leave behind.' Didn't add, *I was a fool*. But I sure felt like it.

I was naïve, that's a constant truth of my life. I never knew one day to the next what kinda thing I was getting into. No idea how I was to live, let alone how to make sure the child in my belly lived. Must be hanging on by both fists, to have survived what we been through already.

'You tryin' to make me intervene in what's coming to you?' Faden leaned forward, elbows on wide thighs.

'Reckon maybe I am. But if you can't or won't, there's something else you can do for me. We got a tradition in my family.'

I tried easing my shoulder up from the cot, but a bolt of pain claimed my ribs. I lay right back down.

'What do I care for your traditions, witch?'

'Somebody's gotta see my son raised. Gotta pass it onto my son, the tradition. Might as well be you.'

If my son had a power, maybe he'd have a power like Webb's. Able to talk to the dead. Then all I'd have to do is see my son born. But I couldn't be sure. We all carry the seeds of our futures in us, I believe that. Swimming in our blood or hardening in our bones. We're the sum of what's coming to us, a skin-moment in a world that is nothing but a string of moments, each one of 'em important to someone. What was important to me then was my son getting his chance at power. Because if history had birthed no other human being like me, well, my son was going to be different again. He'd have his own power and I prayed gods it would be something good.

'You think you gonna live long enough to birth a child? Beating probably end your life before morning, your kid's, too.'

That was just cruel, saying that to a pregnant woman.

'His name is Maxillius.' This through gritted teeth. 'First born boys in my family, but only every second generation. Always Maxillius. And he's gonna have a power.'

'Like his mother?'

'Different, but something.'

'Your power tell you that, witch?'

Would've rolled my eyes if I had it in me. Ain't nothing to do with power, that type of knowledge, except the power that motherhood brings. But I knew, right then, if I was first with a strange kind of power, my son was second. Beyond that I didn't know anything. But knowing that was enough.

Faden made a clicking sound with his tongue. 'Sounds complicated.'

'Takes care of itself. Every second generation, first born is a boy. And his name's gonna be Maxillius. It's the way of things. If I don't make it through, you think you can tell him that for me?'

I'm not no believer but I was praying then or something like it. My son had to live. He had to see his power realised and make a space in the world for people like us. Maybe he'd have his own babes with power. Either way, right then his life was more precious to me than my own and my love for him was something fierce. I hadn't known my own mother, no way to tell if this was normal. Didn't feel it but I'd never had normal. Wasn't sure what it felt like.

'My son's got to live, Faden.'

He didn't answer. He was listening, but not to me. There was a thrumming outside. Horses. A dozen or more.

'Don't suppose I've got a right to hope that's wild horses, lost their heads and about to run through town by accident? Maybe about to knock over this here gaol and set us free?'

'They're not wild,' Faden mutters, 'but their riders are.'

Then he tells me the only useful thing I heard since way before Chella died. He says, 'If I get the chance, I'll see your son right. Born and raised up. And whatever his power, I'll make sure he don't end up where you ended up.'

And that was it. All I could ask. I thanked him, because my power had never lead me anywhere but bad places, and my badness had less to do with my power than it had to do with the world.

The horses stopped and Faden got up to check the window. He eased his belt around his middle and chewed a corner of his mouth.

'What you see, Sheriff?'

'Priest is with them. You could be in luck. Looks like maybe they're bringing food.'

He got back in his seat and waited, half-turned towards the door. There was a rattle of keys and then a man stood in the way of it.

'Bring me the keys!' My voice was hoarse.

The man just looked at me like I was dumb.

'That's Alby,' Faden's voice was like lead. 'He speaks no word of English. I'd says you've got your work cut out for you.'

'He read lips?' I was desperate.

'Don't read, don't speak,' Faden was halfway through explaining, his bulk turning back 'round to face me, when Alby came right up behind him with that heavy tray and thumped Faden in the back of the skull. Right in the place where it must've happened onto his neck. Faden jerked, slid out and hit the floor while Alby danced out of the way.

Faden lay by his upturned chair, shuddering and spasming, drooling out his mouth and bleeding out of his head. Then Alby came at me. He took that tray and slammed it up the side of my temple, me screaming the whole time. But no words coming out.

Next I woke up I was in a place that stank of pigs and vermin. Trussed like a calf, and all. Ankle to ankle, wrist to wrist. I hurt even worse than in Faden's prison. Whole right side of my head throbbed like a fire-toad breathing under my eye. When I got up the courage I reached my hands to it. My face was swollen and pulped, I couldn't even feel bone. But that wasn't the worst of it. Something hard and metal jutted from my shattered cheek. Iron links as long as my knuckles, pulled

91

into a chain. It cut my jaw, passed my teeth and tongue, came out under my eye. And there was clamped with a gate lock.

They'd chained up my voice. Nearly broke my head doing it, whole thing sticky with blood. I tried to speak but all that came out was a grunt like an animal makes. I nearly threw up but was afraid to drown in it. So I bit back, swallowing, breathing shaky through my nose.

'You see here, I got the key?' A new voice, smooth and deep. I squinted at where he stood, sun at his waist. 'My name's Sty, see, and I'm gonna give you the key once a day. So's you can eat. And when we get to where we going, I unlock you and you says what I tells you. Maybe I tells you, "unlock the safe" or "hand over the money" or "drop your guns". And I wad my ears, so's you can't charm me. See? You'll do what I tells you, right?'

He was twirling that key between finger and thumb. Seeing me nod too slow he made to throw it. No way I could follow, so I screams against my chain and set the shattered bone of my face to humming.

'Better. You control with words, woman. But I control with iron. Understood?'

The nodding roiled my head some and the vomit hit the back of my throat. I breathed it down. Sty grinned. Sounded like I was crying but I was just trying to live.

I had me listed as a bad man, but I'd never done bad, not in any kinda way could be intentional. But right then I vowed I'd kill Sty. In his sleep, on the road. I'd find a way. I'd take that key and I'd make him choke on it, I swore that.

First time, then, the baby in my belly kicked.

***

Months and then some. Road looks the same it ever did. All looks like running. Places with no names, people with nothing. Met 'em all before, met 'em all again or someone looked like 'em. Chella said you tired of the road, you tired of living, and still he was right. I was tired of all of it, now even more, with the baby keeping me up at night and Sty tying me upright to my horse.

I did what he told me 'cos I was scared. Simple as that. We lifted bills from banks and travellers, me mouthing his commands through my shattered face in a voice I didn't recognise. Still worked, though. Sty and his gang with their ears wadded up, grinning at me like we was sharing some kinda game. Grinning and winking, mocking me, my right eye so puffed and tortured I couldn't see out of it any more.

Months of going in circles while everything in our path dried up. I wasted around my belly, weight falling off me like water off a roof. But my belly grew and Maxillius in it. Chella haunted me stronger than ever, too. Probably wanted to see his son. Should've asked that Webb while I had the chance, asked if he'd ever heard from Chella. It would've helped me to know, maybe that he was watching over us. As it was, only thing between our child and death was me. I didn't feel good 'bout that.

Maybe that's where my power came from. Maybe some god of children wanted to give Maxillius a chance. Kid had nothing but a dead father and a screwed up mother, and I got to thinking what would happen to him when he was born,

what Sty and the others would do. I couldn't even guess at
that. I didn't want to.

There were a dozen in Sty's posse, I never learned their
names or even if they had 'em. One good thing about being
a witch, they left me alone. Even Sty, though he threatened
otherwise often enough. He was careful our skin didn't
touch, even when he unlocked the chain in my face enough
I could move. The hate in me was like a shield, pushed 'em
all away. Eventually it fell to just Alby to guard me. When
he took off like sometimes he did, they gave the job to some
deaf man, lost his hearing blowing up a bank. He'd sit with
his back to me and talk and talk. That's how I learned most
of what I did about Sty and his team, though all of it I forgot.
Didn't want that knowledge in my skull. Didn't want it in
my baby's blood.

We got back round to where we'd been, some town with
no name or some other town that looked like it. We was on
horses, moving slow, Sty thinking himself right powerful.
Telling us all how he was like a locomotive, fastest, hardest
man in the world. His voice like the bellow of a bull. He
was bragging and cussing, going on about some thing of
his, leaning back on his horse and rubbing his belly. He was
growing thick with success, was Sty. All that good eating
and drinking, earned from my power and what I could do.
His dozen men were laughing like they feared nothing in the
world. Still laughing when the back of Sty's head came off in
a pink cloud. He rolled to one side and fell, foot still caught
in his saddle, hands dragging in the dirt behind what was left
of his head. Whole thing leaving a red smear.

I was so numb with running and starving I forgot even to be glad. Just stared at Sty's open eyes, gathering dust. Alby dropped to my right and three more after that. Still I sat in my saddle, looking round like I was watching a puppet show. Wondering what in hell was going on.

My horse rolled and fell so sudden my legs were in the air when it hit. Saved me from being pinned under. Tied to its neck I hit the ground on shoulder and hip, my belly lurching. The baby inside lurching, too. I had a sharp pain and then felt the warm rush of something wet all over my legs and waist. I thought it was blood but it was too clear.

Hold on, I tells him. Then, *Maxillius, your power is not in your timing.*

Maybe he thought it was gonna be safer out in the world than inside me.

Gunfire was all over. I wondered how I'd missed it 'til then. Road had sapped my will, or Sty had. I lay against my horse like it was a shield, heard the soft yelp of bullets through its hide. No complaint from the horse so I guessed it already gone. I took to the rope at my wrists, working it free with my teeth, keeping my head down behind the horse's neck. Alby was on the ground beside me, bleeding from the gut. He rolled to one side like he was making to sit up. I got a hand free and stretched out to him. I took his gun from his hand—easy 'cos he was weak—and I shot him. Right in the middle of the chest. I had no cause to like Alby, but didn't see no reason to draw out his dying. Just didn't like having him there beside me with a gun in his hands. Too unpredictable, I reckoned.

I got my other hand free and crawled to where Sty lay. My senses were returning to me, enough I felt cheated that I hadn't been the one to kill him. I would've liked it. I started searching for that damn key in every pocket. Found it stuffed into his trousers, in a string on his waist so it must've tapped against his cock when he was riding. It was his final insult, I figured, to hold my imprisonment so close to his lap. Even dead he was a sick son of a bitch.

Guns had stopped, devil only knew what was coming. I jerked the key free and fitted it to the lock on my face. A shadow fell on me while I was twisting it, listening to the click of the bolt. I figured this was probably it, Maxillius wasn't gonna be born after all. Poor kid had come so close. It wasn't right, but plenty in the world isn't right and that doesn't stop it. I cradled the lock with both hands and refused to look up at what was coming next.

Someone spat in the dust to my right. 'Told you I'd see your boy raised.'

Faden, of all people. Just as fat and dumb as I remembered, gods love him for it. His eyes ranged my broken face and he let out a string of blasphemy. He squatted beside me and reached to hold me up, 'cos I was flagging.

Just in time, he was, because my son was churning my belly something fierce. He was on his way into this here world and I was going to tell him a story. All about the life that got lived up 'til his own began. I'd be telling him that story for the rest of my life, however long I got.

Didn't pay no mind to the future until my son arrived. Didn't pay no mind to the past either. But the moment to moment, well, it can kill you. Faden helped me with the lock and eased the chain out of my face for all the hours of screaming and cursing it took. I figured I looked a sight, blood dripping down my shirt and my face throbbing until my skull took over with a thumping all its own.

'You know, that wasn't even a command,' I tells him. 'That was just conversation.'

'About raising your son?' Faden shook his head. 'I'm a man of my word.'

'Next time,' I says, 'don't take so long to live up to your word.'

Faden grins. 'Whatever you say.'

And that was as close to a happy ending as I ever seen.

Cross That Bridge

Ponti approached the house cautiously. No reason for it. He did most things cautiously. His boss told him once his talents were wasted in the police force, he should've tried the army. Ponti was pretty sure he wouldn't pass the physical. Plus, he wasn't a killer, he was a hunter.

In the thick rain the house was as insubstantial as a ghost. It was small, a kind of teacup cottage. Probably a quaint little house once, but it had been let go. The lawn was long, paint was peeling, a couple of old dollhouses sat on the porch, their insides bleached from exposure. It looked like the kind of place a young couple might move to, hoping to start a family. Then the kids come along, the family life gets overwhelming, the couple sour on each other and one of them leaves. Whoever's left outgrows the house without affording to scale up.

Ponti ran through the whole scenario in the brief time it took him to reach the porch.

Out of the rain, he squatted by the dollhouses. Two of them, almost generationally different in their styles. One, plain and functional with square wooden rooms. The other, newer. An ornate plastic thing with broken hinges where a frontage would once have been. Sisters, he surmised, but not alike. About a decade between their ages, too. He filed that away in case it became relevant.

Rain leaked into the collar of his trenchcoat. He knocked on the door, loudly so they could hear over the storm, and the wet skin of his knuckles smarted.

A young uniform answered. Ponti showed her his badge and she threw the door wide. Inside the house was as unkempt as it was outside. That was good. Ponti didn't like surprises.

'The mother's in the kitchen. Father's due any minute,' the uniform told him.

'Alone?'

'No, in the company of a patrol car.'

Ponti hesitated. 'I meant, the mother.'

The uniform—Griegs, her badge read—shrugged. 'We asked if we could call someone. Apparently she doesn't have any friends. That she likes.'

'And the sister?'

'Upstairs, how'd you know?'

'Two dollhouses.' Ponti took a look around the empty lounge room. It was cheap, that was the best description. Plaid lounge in yellow and blue, side tables with no discernible style, the furniture arranged in a semi-circular homage to the television. Candles and faux flowers dotted the surfaces, but mostly they were faded and dusty.

'Wait.' Griegs pointed the corner of her notebook at him. 'Ponti. You're *that* Detective Ponti, aren't you? The one that finds lost kids.'

'Unless there's two of us.'

Griegs sized him up. Ponti figured her for detective material from that look alone. 'That boy you found at Myall Lakes—how'd you do it?'

'Do what?'

'For one thing, he was snatched from Campbelltown. So, how'd you know to take a five hour road trip north while everyone else was still door-knocking his neighbours? Seems kinda…'

'Strange? Yeah, well,' Ponti acknowledged, 'I didn't say it wasn't strange.'

Danny Lin was the kid's name. Eight years old. Broke his arm once climbing onto his garage roof, but apart from that no harm had ever come to Danny in his entire short life. Not until his family drove home from the children's hospital, tailed by two paedophiles. Robert Olsen and Michael Klei snatched Danny that night and drove him north to their campsite where at least four other adults waited. What happened to Danny overnight was difficult to piece together. And the only witnesses were too riddled with illegal substances to be sure of it themselves. But what happened next was a young officer by the name of Ponti followed an invisible trail to a cold campsite fire, where the burned body of Danny Lin waited. Danny was identified by the compound fracture in his left forearm, set less than twenty-four hours earlier and easily recalled by the attending doctor.

Ponti hadn't needed the identification, he'd known it was Danny. His first and most famous case. He'd felt like a puppet on a string, following a strange ache in his sternum, a stinging in his skin. Over time he'd grown used to this peculiar reaction. Had even learned to be grateful for it. He'd seen bad things in his time, but a missing kid, that was the worst thing he could imagine. At least he had something to offer through his strange power.

Ponti tracked the kiddy fiddlers, too. He didn't need supernatural powers to find those guys, just raw, hard detective work. Took him years, but he didn't stop. He couldn't. The memory of standing over Danny's body was always with him, even now.

He hadn't known it at the time, but he'd had only hours left of his ordinary life. After Danny's discovery there was the questioning and local suspicion and a newly nervous police command trying to wrap up his career right alongside the case. Nobody liked his inexplicable ability to find missing children. It tarred him. He got himself a reputation for being creepy and also psychic. But mostly creepy. Of course, when the missing kid cases kept coming in, they called him first. Ponti never said no, despite the increasing suspicions of his colleagues. Let them go through everything he owned. Ponti was clean.

'If my partner shows up, let her in,' Ponti said.

'Thought you worked alone.'

'Not by choice.'

In the kitchen the mother hunched in a chair and stared at the table edge. Her posture was slack but her hands were rigid in her lap. Ponti took a seat opposite and waited until her eyes rolled around to meet his. It took a while, but he had time. The ache in his sternum wasn't there, or the prickling in his scalp. Until he knew more about the missing girl—until he knew her as a human being, not just as a case title—he had nothing to do but wait.

'Take your coat?' the mother asked. Her voice was low and gruff. Fear and cigarettes, Ponti figured, fear and liquor.

'I'm fine.'

'No,' she placed her hands flat on the table and levered herself up. 'Take your coat. You're raining on my furniture.'

'Oh.' Ponti relinquished the coat and sat back on the wet chair.

'When did you last see your daughter, Mrs—'

'You mean Angelique?'

Parents of missing kids always used their names like loaded weapons. If they didn't, they were guilty.

'When did you last see Angelique?'

Pretentious name for an ordinary suburb like St Peters. Smacked of people yearning to break free, people who'd gotten pregnant too early, sacrificed their dreams, figured they'd live vicariously through their children for the rest of their lives. Angelique, it transpired, went missing after dinner last evening, sometime between nine and dawn. Came home, ate, went to her room, put on some music, was heard talking and laughing on the phone. She was six, but her mother took pains to explain she was independent.

'Still, she's young for her own phone,' Ponti said.

'It's the house phone. We make sure she has some family numbers programmed. Her dad, her grandparents. I can pick up anytime and listen in.'

'Did you?'

103

'Maybe once or twice. I went to bed early.'

'Who was she talking to?'

'Her Gramma.'

'What was the conversation like?'

She shrugged. 'The usual. When are you coming to visit, when can I visit you?'

'From Gramma? Or from Angelique?'

'Both. Peas in a pod, those two.'

'So, what were the answers?'

'That we're too broke for a trip to Exmouth, and Gramma is too old to fly.' She pulled out a cigarette and rolled it between her fingers. 'Well, those weren't the answers. But they're the reasons.'

'Exmouth in England?'

'Yeah, that Exmouth,' she said in that scratchy voice.

Ponti shifted his weight. 'Has Angelique ever disappeared before?'

'Never.' The cigarette was between her lips now but she hadn't lit it. Probably trying to quit. Probably didn't trust her hands not to shake.

'Mrs Thomas, what's your relationship with Angelique like?'

'That's not my name.' She gave him a look that could put out a light globe. 'And we have a typical loving mother-daughter relationship.'

Ponti wanted to ask, 'Typical—or loving?' In his experience, there was no typical with parental relationships. Each one was unique. 'What name should I use for you, ma'am?'

'Naomi will do fine. Don't need my husband's name,

don't need my father's name. Just, Naomi.'

'So, Naomi, you were close with Angelique?'

'Of course.'

'What's the name of her best friend at school?'

'Melissa,' she said without hesitation.

That didn't prove anything. Most schools had a couple of Melissas.

There was noise in the hallway. The father had arrived, two uniforms in tow. He was a slight man in a mechanic's dark blue shirt and trousers. His bald head made him look mean, and so did the tattoos on his upper arms. One, a serpent that wrapped all the way from elbow to shirt sleeve. The other, something Celtic, plaited symbols that crowded his forearm. His hands hung loose at his sides, curved like he was still holding tools.

'Oh, my God,' he recited like a litany. 'Oh my God.'

He stalled in the middle of the room and looked from Naomi to Griegs to Ponti. He was distraught. Looked genuine. He looked scared, too, like he expected the worst. Ponti made a mental note of his dazed distress and the ex-wife's flat contempt. Could be nothing, but it paid to know these things. He filed it away with the dollhouses. The real detective work was figuring out which details mattered.

'Griegs, can you take Mr Thomas' statement? I'll sit in.'

They moved to the lounge room under the dark gaze of the ex-Mrs Thomas. Probably didn't want the cops traipsing through her house with her ex-husband, probably didn't want rain on her carpet. Probably didn't want her daughter gone.

Thomas sat rigid on the edge of the lounge. Ponti examined him again, head to toe. Could be hiding something, but probably not hiding his daughter. Right then and for no reason he was ever able to articulate, Ponti was sure of it. Most cops called it a gut instinct. For Ponti it was something more.

'When did you last see your daughter?' Griegs flipped open her notebook.

'Week and a half ago, last visit Naomi let me have.'

'Not gotten around to custody rights yet?' Ponti asked.

'Not yet,' Thomas clenched his hands. 'Speak to her every night on the phone, though. Spoke to her last night.'

'What time was that?' Griegs cut back in.

Ponti remembered he'd asked her to run this interview. He leaned back.

'I don't know, ten, ten-thirty.'

'Usual for her to be up so late, Mr Thomas?' Griegs prompted. 'She was six.'

'Six in two weeks,' Thomas gazed around the room for something familiar, but didn't seem to find it. Ponti figured nothing was familiar when the world was upside down.

'Mr Thomas, may I ask,' Ponti interrupted, 'how was her mood?'

'She…' Thomas trailed off.

'Was she cheerful, sad, angry?'

'She was angry. And sad. She wanted to visit her Gramma, but no one can afford a trip like that right now.'

'Did she get on with her mother?'

Thomas' gaze locked on Ponti. He recognised the look.

'Anything you say doesn't leave this room, Mr Thomas.'

'Kids,' Thomas said slowly. 'They grow up fast these days. Used to be you'd be a teenager before you started needing your independence, you know? But now … I mean, it's not all Naomi's fault. The girls are just … they're a handful.'

'How so?'

'Angie, she's always sneaking out, disappearing. Found her down the shopping centre in the middle of the night once. Whole place was locked up, alarm was on. Don't even know how she got inside. Naomi blamed me. I'd had a few drinks, sure, but … I'm not stupid. I don't let five year olds out of the house in the dark. And I can't break into a locked shopping centre.'

It wasn't lost on Ponti that he'd just been told by Angie's mother that she never disappeared. 'And your other daughter?'

'Vegetarian.'

'You suggested both your kids were a handful, Mr Thomas. Do you have any other details?'

'When you've got a lot going on, Detective, a detail like that is enough.'

Ponti acknowledged the remark with a nod. 'What's Naomi's reaction to all this?'

'She sleeps. A lot.'

'Kids must feel she's become distant.'

'They probably do, yeah. She'll get through. She's strong, they all are.'

'So, you think Angie ran away this time?'

'No.'

'How can you be sure?'

'Because she always comes back. Or she phones, or she tells me where she's going. Even the shopping centre, she told me where she was going. I just didn't believe her.'

Some kids couldn't be held, not by anything. Ponti reflected if the kid had a knack for getting out of a locked house into a locked, alarmed shopping centre, she could be anywhere. Still nothing called to him, tried to lift the skin from his body or drag his sternum forward. No sign, yet, of Angie.

'I'd like to see her room.'

Thomas gestured to the stairway. 'Second on the right.'

The phone rang and Ponti froze halfway to his feet. 'Do we have this line bugged yet?'

Griegs already had her walkie talkie to her ear. 'I'm checking.'

Ponti crossed the room towards the kitchen. Naomi was hanging over the table like her whole body was a question mark. 'Should I answer it?'

Ponti nodded. 'If there's any demands, I'll take over.'

'You think it's kidnappers?'

Ponti tried not to look around the plain, functional room he was standing in. In his experience kidnappers didn't take kids from houses where the paint was peeling, not for ransom. Those kids were taken for good. But he didn't tell Naomi that.

'Answer it, and we'll find out.'

Naomi reached for the receiver. When she got it to her ear, her voice had lost its gruffness. 'Hello?'

Ponti leaned in, every muscle tense. Thomas had entered the room and stood in front of them, flexing his fists and making his tattoos roll. Ponti heard the voice of an old woman on the other end of the line. It was so unexpected it took him a moment to make out the words.

'Dearie, we've been having such a lovely time. Haven't we, sweetie? It's been a wonderful surprise.'

She had a British accent and a hollow echo to her voice.

'Mum?' Naomi asked.

Ponti felt the energy drain out of him. He took the phone. 'I'm sorry, ma'am, we need this line.'

He tried to cap his frustration. Beside him, Thomas apparently tried and failed. He swore savagely and at length.

'For God's sake, Naomi, get off the damn phone in case she calls!'

'Who's that, darling?' came the old woman's voice down the line. 'Is that Ken?' Then, more muffled, 'Do you want to talk to your Daddy, sweetheart?'

Ponti froze. 'Ma'am, who are you talking to?'

'Do you mean me? Who's that?' the old woman sounded confused.

'Ma'am—'

Naomi interrupted. 'Didn't you hear what she said? Angelique's there. With her.'

'That's right, dearie, she's right here. Shall I put her on?'

'Yes,' Ponti said through gritted teeth. 'Put Angelique on the phone, if she's with you.'

His skin twitched. He could feel the pulse at the side of his temple. This was it, the dawning of that super-sense that would lead him to the little girl. He covered the mouthpiece with a hand and held the phone out to Thomas.

'I need you to tell me if this is your daughter.'

Thomas nodded. He took the phone and held it like he was afraid of breaking it. Ponti crossed to where Griegs stood, to give Thomas some room.

'So maybe the kid just ran away after all?' Griegs asked.

'You remember where Gramma lives, though, right?'

'Not the grandmother in Exmouth?' She looked surprised, then thoughtful. She turned her back so the parents couldn't see what she was saying and dropped her voice. 'There's another explanation, of course.'

Ponti was interested. 'The call's a fake?'

'Or the kid is.'

'I've seen people lie,' Ponti said. 'It doesn't look like this.'

'Parents want to believe—'

'But they also know better than anyone.' His chest had begun to hurt, his skin rippled under his shirt. 'Besides, I know. It's her.'

Naomi had sunk to her chair again, tears rolling down her face. Her ex-husband stood rigid, veins popping in his forehead.

'Angie, honey, it's Daddy. Are you okay?' He listened, then said, 'Is that right? Sweetie? Can you tell Daddy how you got to Gramma's?'

Ponti stepped in, gesturing for Thomas' attention. Thomas looked straight through him but he nodded. It was her. His daughter was on the phone.

'Sir, may I speak with your daughter a moment?'

Thomas was reluctant to hand over the phone. 'Sweetie, it's okay, you can tell Daddy.' He listened, eyes roaming the room. 'Just like that, honey?'

Ponti gestured. 'Sir?'

'Oh, Gramma's saying the call's expensive? Tell her we'll call you right back, sweetie. But first this nice policeman needs to talk to you.' He handed Ponti the phone. 'It's her, it's Angie.' He was grinning with relief and running his hand through his hair, but he was crying, too. 'My God, it's her.'

Ponti covered the mouthpiece. 'You told me you spoke to her around ten o'clock last night, Mr Thomas. That's,' he checked his watch, 'less than eleven hours ago. Last I checked, a flight to London was still fifteen hours. And that's not counting the trip to Exmouth.'

'So, what're you saying? We're lying?' Thomas looked wild.

'I'll need to be convinced otherwise.' He looked over his shoulder to Griegs. 'Check flights for six year old kids, unaccompanied or otherwise. And give local constabulary there a call.'

'I don't think I have any authority over British cops,' she replied.

'Then be polite.' Ponti raised the phone to his ear. 'Is that Angie? Hey, Angie, it's Detective Ponti here.'

'Hello sir.' A child's voice. A formal politeness her parents must have instilled in her. They'd done something right, those two.

'Angie, can you tell me how you got to Gramma's?'

'I told Dad,' she sounded reluctant, like she knew it wasn't going to be believed. 'Through the wardrobe.'

'That's great, Angie. How'd you do that?'

'Daddy says, if you want something really hard, wish for it.'

'That's it, huh? You got in the wardrobe and wished really hard. And then … what happened, exactly?'

'There was a doorway and long bridge and I walked until I was at Gramma's house.'

'What did Gramma do when she saw you?'

'She cried. She thought I was a ghost. But then I told her I came through the wardrobe, she said it was like a fairytale.'

'Okay, Angie. Thanks for talking to me.'

He handed the phone back to Naomi and looked away while she rocked and cried and spoke to her daughter.

'I'm going to check out the girl's room. You got a partner here with you?'

'Had to send her home sick,' Griegs replied. 'Food poisoning. I'll stay here with the parents.'

Ponti nodded acknowledgement and headed for the stairs. On the way, he pulled out the phone number for his new partner. She picked up on the first ring.

'Palmer.'

'Detective Enora Palmer?'

'Yeah, who's this?'

'Detective Maxillius Ponti.'

'Welcome aboard. You got my message?'

'You said to call if I came across something weird?'

'Sounds like you did?'

'A six-year-old girl who ran away to Gramma's place.'

A pause. 'I admit, I was expecting more. Unless the grand-mother's, I don't know, dead?'

'That's a harsh thing to say about Exmouth.'

'Gramma's in Exmouth?'

'And the girl ran away through a magic wardrobe.'

'That's more like it,' Palmer's voice warmed. 'Where are you?'

He gave her the address. Near the top of the stairs he spotted Angie's sister. She was at least twelve years older than Angie, teenaged and darkly dressed—emo or goth, he'd never learned the difference. Her face was carefully made up to look pasty-white, but the thick black kohl around her eyes was smeared to grey shadows.

'I gotta go, Palmer.' He hung up the phone. To the girl, he said, 'I'm Detective Ponti. You must be…?'

If she understood the question, she didn't show it. Two more steps from where he stood, a door was ajar. An embroi-dered pink nameplate pronounced it the residence of Jade.

'That's your room, right? Jade?' Still no answer. 'Your sister is on the phone if you want to talk to her.'

He was keenly aware that he couldn't interview a minor alone.

'Where is she this time, Angie?'

Her voice was surprisingly deep. Ponti reflected she'd probably sing great jazz in a few years. 'Your mum and dad will explain. Do you mind if I call the officer over here?'

Jade shook her head and Ponti called out for Griegs. She came quickly, eyeing Jade in the corridor. With Griegs beside him, Ponti asked Jade if she'd be willing to answer some questions. 'What time was it when you last saw your sister?'

'Last night, at dinner.'

'And then, what happened after that?'

'She went to her room. She's easy to track. Always singing or on the phone. Or talking to herself.'

'Handy,' Ponti observed.

'Yeah,' Jade agreed drily. 'It's mostly great.'

'She has an active imagination, then?'

'Yeah, that's great, too.'

'Has she run away before?'

Jade shrugged. 'Nobody wants to talk about it. It's too weird.'

'Weird is my bread and butter,' Ponti assured her.

'Angie … doesn't run. She just disappears. And then she reappears some other place. Always comes back, though.'

'Mind if I check her room?'

'They've done that already.'

'Might help me understand.'

Jade shrugged. Ponti edged up the last two stairs and past her, towards the second door. The word 'Angelique' was embroidered in the middle of a forest scene on a homemade nameplate. He'd seen a lot of kids' rooms and this one was typical, crammed with so many stuffed toys and dolls he wondered how the little girl could fit. The walls were painted in shades of purple and blue, decorated with sequins and shells and white-limned furnishings. The bed was messy, the pillows piled high and plump. But no imprint of a little girl's head.

Jade followed him in. 'What're you looking for?'

'A wardrobe.'

'Guess you found one, then?'

The wardrobe doors hung open, revealing a rainbow of clothes on thick plastic hangers. The shoes were scuffed and there was the unmistakable smell of old washing. Looked like only her name was fancy. Ponti knelt by the wardrobe and leaned in. Funny how the back of the wardrobe hadn't been limned white like the doors. On closer inspection he realised it was a dark stain like a small explosion. He moved the shoes aside so he could kneel inside. There was no sign of chemicals or charcoal, no residual warmth, no warp in the wood. Just a plain, black stain.

Jade came to crouch beside him.

'I'm going to have to ask you to step back.' Ponti held his arm out straight in front of her, trying to block her. 'I need to investigate the scene. Griegs?'

'What scene? This is a wardrobe.'

Jade leaned in as if to prove it, reaching her hand to the dark stain at the back. The air crackled like lightning and a spark leapt from the wardrobe to her hand, bright in the dark interior. Griegs grabbed the girl's shoulders and pulled her back. Jade collapsed to the floor, eyes fixed on her hand. She flexed her fingers and rubbed at her skin. It was unmarked.

'What just happened?' Griegs asked.

'There's something in there,' Jade said. 'I felt it.'

Ponti felt it, too.

'Griegs, take Jade to her parents, please.'

When they left he sat on the floor surrounded by pastel little girl's things, making him feel like an old, grey giant.

He soaked up everything there was to know about Angie Thomas in that room. The hairbrush and comb on her dressing table, the game of Connect 4, its contents scattered on the floor by her bed, the clothes piled by the door, the hairbands with gem-like butterflies and spiders and ladybugs lined up in rows in an old cutlery tray on a low bookshelf. The photo of a blonde girl on a swing with her mother behind her, both of them grinning into the sun, caught at the point when the swing was going to rush backwards out of the sky. He felt that ache in his sternum like an arrow. He looked at the wardrobe, but was afraid to touch it.

'Detective Ponti, I take it?'

A tall woman stood over him, long hair pulled back, shoulders straight. She wore jogging clothes and her rich skin had a sheen of sweat.

'Palmer? Did you jog here?'

'It was meant to be my day off.'

'Sorry about that.'

'I'm used to it. This the wardrobe in question?'

'Listen,' Ponti stalled. 'I owe you some thanks. Haven't had a partner in a lot of years. Most people find me too creepy.'

'I get that.' She cast a glance around the room, taking it all in. 'People don't want to partner with me either. But for different reasons.'

The kind of scandal that had followed Palmer would have put paid to a lesser career. But rumour had it she'd found some powerful backers lately, and not necessarily in the force. She could pick any partner she wanted, even 'that kiddy freak' Max Ponti. She leaned into the wardrobe before he could stop her, and rapped a knuckle on the thin plywood, outside and then inside the stain. A spark shot across her hand and Palmer let out a shout.

'Sorry, should've warned you.'

Palmer blew on her hand like she was cooling it. 'Should've asked.'

Ponti reached for the stain. A surge of energy grabbed for him, hauling him forward. His fingers disappeared to the knuckles, as neatly as if they'd been sliced off. An ache travelled the bones of his hands up to his shoulder and across, making every bone a conduit for some dark pain.

He snatched his hand away and rocked back, out of the wardrobe. He'd often felt like his skin would lift from his body, that wasn't new. But he'd never had the feeling that his bones might shoot out of his skin. It hurt, and it frightened him, and he wasn't sure he wanted to feel that again.

'Okay,' Palmer steadied him with a hand to his shoulder, 'how'd you do that?'

'That's how Angie disappeared. She travelled along this whatever-it-is, this *magnet*. She probably built it, used it to draw her towards where she wanted to go.'

'You're rambling,' Palmer observed. 'Let's try again. How did *you*—'

'It's this thing I do. Connect to missing kids and follow them. Because I connected to Angie, I can follow her. It's … hard to explain.'

'I think that's all the explanation I need.'

Palmer was patient, he gave her that. She crouched, waiting, plait hanging over one shoulder, hands flat against each other. She was watching him with a light on in her eyes.

'I'm okay,' he said. 'You ever seen anything this strange?'

She spread her hands. 'There's no rating scale for weird. But if this kid can make a doorway to wherever she wants to go, she could be the most powerful person I'm likely to meet. And I've met some powerful people.'

'Great.' Ponti sat back on his heels.

'So. You going to follow Angie down this particular rabbit hole?'

Ponti hesitated.

'That's why we're here, right?' Palmer asked.

'I'm not sure about this one,' Ponti said.

'Because you don't fancy a free trip to England?'

'Because I've felt what's waiting beyond this wall, ready to pull me apart.'

Palmer seemed to wait. 'And what is that?'

Ponti chewed his lip and thought and rubbed at the fingers that had disappeared into the wall. They felt like they'd been scalded. 'I don't know.'

'Well, Detective Ponti,' Palmer said, 'seems to me you've got a gift. A power. And with great power ... well, you know the rest.'

'Don't tell me. Something about responsibility, right?'

She nodded, smiled. On Palmer, a smile was something bittersweet. 'I knew we'd make a good team.'

Ponti watched the wardrobe. 'This isn't how I normally do this thing.'

'You find lost kids, right? You find them and you bring them home.'

'Yeah.'

'Whatever it costs you?'

'I've been meaning to review that bit.'

'Well,' Palmer eased to her feet, 'this lost kid isn't home yet. So. What're you going to do?'

Ponti hesitated. He felt like he'd gone into a store for dental floss and come out with barbed wire. He thought of Jade, of the Thomases downstairs probably reconciling over their daughter's mysterious flight. He thought about Palmer's offer, to be her partner and work the weird cases. He thought about the strange phone call he'd received the other day, from a man claiming he'd been in touch with Ponti's grandparents from beyond the grave, and the job offer the man had made. A contract for something called the Grey Institute, to hone his skills for 'whatever you want', the man had said.

He thought about his job as a police detective, his fractured career and the open case on the disappearance of Angelique Thomas. He figured he could throw in the towel right now.

'Who am I kidding?' he asked. 'I'm going in.'

'Of course you are.' Palmer slapped his shoulder.

He leaned forward and tested his fingers against the energy beyond the wall. He moved carefully, his arm lengthening and stretching, his bones feeding into the space like spaghetti down a drain pipe. For a brief, terrifying moment he thought maybe he wouldn't all fit, maybe this magnetic space was built for six-year-olds, maybe he'd be forever divided between this world and whatever was beyond it. A stinging sensation crawled across his body, drawing him in.

'One more thing.' Palmer still had her hand on his back, like she might comfort him. 'Be careful.'

Ponti opened his mouth to reply and Palmer shoved him hard into the wardrobe.

Every cell of his body *whooshed* out in rapid-fire dissolution. He was scattered by whatever held him. The darkness in that place weighed more than he did, much more. It was crushing him to an almost-paste. He was nothing but a froth of cells, unconnected except that they were pushed by the same tide. He focused on Angie and let himself be drawn.

When at last his fingers brushed something solid, he hooked both hands on it and pulled himself through. He was in a wardrobe in a room with red carpet and a pair of unmade beds, the mattresses bare. He smelled mothballs and linen. A guest room, then, mostly unused.

'Angie?'

His insides hurt. His all-of-him hurt, throbbed and ached from his eardrums to the skin under his toenail. His sternum hurt worst of all and for a moment he thought he was having a heart attack. He hoped it meant, instead, that Angie was here. Close by. Behind him the wardrobe was unmarked. No sign of his passage through there, or Angie's. No obvious way back. He would've cursed Palmer if he hadn't been so pleased to be alive. He rubbed at his chest and steadied himself with a hand against the wall. He stood a moment, pulling himself together.

A nearby phone startled him, until he realised it was his own phone, in his pocket. Well, holy crap. If his phone was fine maybe the rest of him was fine, too. Palmer's number flashed on the screen.

'Thank God,' she said when he answered. 'I've been calling for two hours.'

'It's been that long?' He checked his watch. No wonder it had taken Angie hours to phone home. If time stretched during the journey, she might have just gotten here. 'Tell me you didn't push me into that wardrobe as some kind of physics experiment.'

'I was helping you meet your destiny,' Palmer replied. 'Besides, I failed science at school. Are you okay?'

'I think so.'

'Why are you whispering?'

'I don't know where I am. I don't know who else is here.'

'Aren't you at Gramma's place?'

Ponti stepped into a corridor so narrow the walls seemed to be leaning in. He could hear voices. 'Maybe. Stay with me.'

'I'm not going anyplace,' she assured him.

Ponti followed the voices to a sitting room. A lounge suite with a pink floral design, carpets worn to grey. An old woman, her face creased along with her soft, faded clothes. And beside her a young girl with messy blonde hair and a grin.

'Angie?'

Ponti stepped into the room and stopped hard. Not from choice. Something had him by the left shoulder, some burning thing that, for a moment, he thought might be the space, the magnet, the *whatever* he'd travelled to get here.

His arm was numb, he couldn't lift it. The phone was some-place on the floor and he was staring at Angie, that startled little girl who looked like she was screaming though he couldn't hear a thing over the roar in his ears.

He reached his other hand to his shoulder and felt wet heat pulse through his fingers.

'Mother of God,' he said. 'I've been shot.'

A new voice, shouting, 'I said *get to your knees!*'

Ponti wondered if the new voice meant him. He lowered himself to his knees to be sure. 'I've been shot, *goddammit*.'

Could they hear him? His phone was by his knee, Palmer shouting his name. The world spun and danced and he felt sweat break out on his face. Someone grabbed his uninjured shoulder and pushed, carefully but methodically, until he was lying flat on the ground, hand pinned beneath him still holding his shoulder. Weight was put on his good shoulder to hold him there.

He could hear cries from others in the room, the old woman and young girl. He wondered from far away whether he'd walked into a home invasion.

Face pressed to the carpet, he said, 'Detective Ponti, New South Wales Police.'

If they were going to kill him for being a cop, they may as well do it quickly. The way he was feeling, it would be a kind of blessing.

Quiet from behind him. 'You're not meaning South Wales, then, are you?'

'Australia,' he confirmed, voice muffled even to his own ears.

'You've got ID?'

'If you get off me, I'll show you.'

The weight lifted from his shoulder. Ponti was helped first to his knees and then his feet. On the carpet was a red stain where his shoulder would have been, visible even on the red carpet.

'You shot me.'

'No comment,' said the British uniform. He had dark skin and hair shaved so short he was almost bald. He wore a dark blue jumpsuit with yellow lettering on the back that Ponti couldn't quite catch, even though the man was side on. And, apparently, he carried a gun.

'I thought British cops didn't use guns,' Ponti said. Then, 'You *shot* me.'

'Counter Terrorism, mate. We get guns in Counter Terrorism.'

Outside the lounge room, red and blue lights rolled. Ponti could make out at least half a dozen police cars through the sheer curtains. People moved back and forth among the lights and he heard a rabble of voices at the front door. They'd pulled out all the stops on this one. 'What's this case got to do with terrorism?'

'Classified.'

Ponti looked over at Angie, her face screwed up with fear. If he got her out of this, she'd probably have to go to ground. That, or be earmarked as a national security risk in almost every country she could reach.

The Counter Terrorism cop raised a walkie talkie to his face. 'Send an ambulance. Minor flesh wound.'

'Minor?'

'Just grazed you, mate. I've seen worse.'

Ponti pulled his badge free with his good hand and held it out. The Counter Terrorism cop probably hadn't only seen worse. Probably done worse, too. 'So, now you know my name.'

'DSI Venables,' said the cop. 'Mind answering how you got here?'

'Same way Angie did.' He gestured to his phone on the floor. 'Could you hand me my phone, DSI?'

Venables retrieved the phone and held it out. To Palmer's credit, she hadn't stopped shouting. He had to hold the phone at arm's distance to avoid being deafened. The blood had begun to congeal on his hand, making the phone tacky. 'I'm okay. Mostly.'

She stopped shouting. 'What happened?'

'Counter Terrorism is on the scene. And, I've been shot. Apparently it's minor.'

Palmer let out a string of expletives. 'How in hell did you get yourself shot?'

'You're the one who shoved me into the wardrobe,' Ponti said through gritted teeth. He regretted it instantly, even before Palmer fell silent. From what he'd gathered about Palmer, her last partner had been shot, too. Worse than him.

'I'm sorry,' he said.

He heard her take a breath. 'Yeah, me too.'

'So, once we get you patched up,' DSI Venables cut in, 'how do you plan to get little miss here home to Sydney, Australia?'

Ponti reflected that was a good question, but he was saved from answering by the arrival of the ambulance. He looked helplessly between the two paramedics to where Angie sat with her Gramma. She looked tired and scared, her gaze fixed on Ponti's wounded shoulder.

'Hi, Angie, do you remember me? We talked on the phone. Detective—ow! Detective Ponti. Maxillius—Max. I'm Max.'

Her eyes flickered to his face and back to his shoulder. 'I remember.'

Gramma pulled Angie in close. 'You plan to take Angie home to her mum and dad?'

She gave Ponti the same kind of glare her daughter had given him back in her St Peters' home. Ponti figured there was power there, in this family. Mostly unexpressed, but still available. Ready for the kind of existential challenge Angie had felt, perhaps, alone in her room one night, wanting desperately to be someplace else. Some place very specific and well-known to her.

'It's my job,' Ponti apologised. He looked at the little girl. Her eyes had welled up with tears. 'Angie, tell me. Did you know you'd be able to travel to Gramma's house like that?'

'Nope.'

'It just happens? You can't control it?'

She nodded.

'I have problems like that,' Ponti assured her. 'Like, when I followed you through the wardrobe. I couldn't control it, either.'

'You can follow me?'

'Sure. It's what I do.'

She gave him a broad grin, obviously figuring him for a comrade in arms. 'Sometimes I just want to be someplace enough. Daddy says, it's bad to want something that much.'

Ponti reflected he was probably right, but it seemed a shame. The girl had a gift. She couldn't control it yet, but that was no reason to deny it. He wondered again about that strange phone call from the Grey Institute. 'Is everything okay at home?'

She nodded, shrugged. A regular little kid in a regular little life whose only problem was that she was bored. And she had a power to address that.

'Angie. Any chance you might be building a bridge back home sometime soon?'

Angie sighed, resting against her Gramma. She gave Ponti's question due consideration, yawned and said, 'Nope.'

Years later, having circumnavigated international politics more than once—though never with as much difficulty as in the Angelique Thomas case—Ponti picked up his phone and placed a call. The recipient let it ring out almost entirely before answering. Times like this he could still feel the old shoulder wound twinge. Phone calls and stormy weather, that's what set it off.

'Hello?' came a voice down the line.

Angie's voice on the other end was older, with just the same amount of confidence she'd always had. But something new, too. Something blasé and dislocated and inevitably teenaged.

'Detective Ponti here, Angie.'

At that point her voice warmed. 'Oh, hey, Max. You know no one calls me that anymore, right?'

'Right. Sorry, Abbey.' Her name ever since her family had gone into protective custody. Not police custody, though. Something bigger. Funded by people who wanted to protect her from the interests of counter terrorists and terrorists equally.

'How's the Grey Institute treating you, Abbey?'

'I can't complain. How are you, Max? Still hunting lost children?'

Testing out her maturity by calling him by his first name. Testing out his acceptance. 'You bet. How could I give up on a vocation like that?'

'Sure. Until they lock you up for being a fruitloop.'

'There's always that option.'

'You still got the same partner?'

'For now.'

He looked over to where Palmer sat at her desk, typing up a report with her usual amount of swearing. She never had learned to type. Through the phone he could hear traffic, the noise of buses, an announcement like at a train station, but in a language he didn't understand. He thought maybe German. Abbey had been travelling for most of a year by now, but the traditional way. Backpacking around Europe.

'What, she going someplace, your partner?' Abbey asked.

He moved away so he could talk privately. 'She's thinking about a job. At the Grey Institute.'

Palmer had been offered that job a lot of times, but she kept turning it down. Said she could do better work as a cop. Ponti had to admit, he couldn't imagine police work without her anymore. But one day, he figured, the Grey Institute would find just the right button to push to score Detective Enora Palmer.

'Wow, that's pretty elite,' said Angie. 'What can she do?'

Ponti knew what she meant. *What's her power, her gift, her strange and precious thing that only she can do, that only she can put into the world?*

'I guess,' he said, 'she brings out the best in people.'

'Oh. Well, that's cool, I guess.'

'We all got something, hey, Abbey?' He shifted his weight. 'What about you? Still travelling in that special way of yours?'

'Nah, not for a while, now. I guess I outgrew it.'

'Do you miss it?'

'Nope. Well, maybe. I mean, it was scary and weird and, no one really knew what to do about it. Not even the Institute.'

'But it was yours.'

'Exactly.' She paused a long time. 'Yeah, I miss it.'

'Maybe it'll be back,' Ponti said. 'Or, maybe it's moved out of the way in order to make room for something else.'

'Think so?'

'Sure, why not?' he said with more confidence than he felt. Who knew how the power ran, where it came from or where it went? 'It's probably just lost for a while. I got a hunch about you, Abbey. Only good stuff is gonna happen in your life.'

She laughed. 'Hey, don't go wasting your hunches on me, Max. I'm already found, remember?'

'I like to think none of us is so found we can't sometimes get a little lost.' He grinned. He was becoming quite the philosopher in his old age. 'Anyhow, I'll keep an eye out for you, Abbey. Just in case.'

'You do that for all your found kids?'

Most of them, Ponti reflected. 'When I can.'

'Your phone bills must be huge.'

'Yeah,' he conceded.

'You don't have to, you know.'

'I know.'

A begrudging tone from a kid who wasn't quite grown but wanted to be. 'Well, it's not like I can stop you.'

Life hadn't given Ponti a whole lot of choices, but it had given him this one. He would use his power—all his powers—in whatever damn way he could, to help whoever he could help. His smarts, his compassion and most of all that strange instinct that could lead him miles in any direction searching for a kid that needed finding. It was either that or let his power use him. That was the bad power, the stuff that couldn't be controlled. Even no power was better than that. Even Angie's power, which she hadn't yet learned to own, to shape, to call her own. Even a power that was lost for a while.

'Well, I got a train to catch,' she said over the noise of a loudspeaker. 'Bruges is next.'

'Hey, that's great. Well, have a great time. See you, Angie.'

'See you, Max.'

He reflected later, after he'd hung up, that even if Angie's power was truly lost, maybe there'd be something else, some strange thing that only she could do. Something she was best at. And if that turned out to be just that she was best at being Angie, he figured that should probably be enough. He'd tell her that, too, when he next called her.

He returned to his desk and started going through his mail. A familiar grey envelope fell out.

'Hey, Palmer?' He held it up. 'I blame you for this.'

Palmer turned, recognised the envelope and gave a chuckle.

'They'll never stop, you know. The Grey Institute. That Webb kid has a special interest in you since chatting with your dead Gramma.'

'So he says. Although, if you believe him it's more like my great-great-great—'

'I get it.'

Ponti hesitated. 'If a week went by without a job offer from Grey—'

'Yeah. I'd miss it, too.'

'One of these days, I just might take it,' he waved the envelope at her.

Palmer went back to her typing. 'You and me both, Detective.'

About the Author

Deborah Biancotti's 2009 publication from Twelfth Planet Press, *A Book of Endings*, was shortlisted for the William L. Crawford Award for Best First Fantasy Book. She is an Aurealis and Ditmar Award winning writer whose work has appeared in *Clockwork Phoenix*, *Eidolon 1*, *Ideomancer*, *infinity plus*, *Australian Dark Fantasy And Horror* and Prime's *Year's Best Dark Fantasy and Horror*. Most recently her critical essay on *No Country for Old Men* as a modern gothic story appeared in Scarecrow Press's *Twenty-First Century Gothic*. Her first novella is upcoming in *Ishtar* from Gilgamesh Press, and she is working on her first and second novels.

This is her first story suite.

Praise for *A Book of Endings*

Shortlisted for the William L. Crawford Award for Best First Fantasy Book.

Nominated for the Aurealis Award for Best Collection.

Listed in the Locus Recommended Reading for 2009, *SF Signal*'s '40 Books from 2009 That You Should Read' and *i09*'s Picks for 2008-09.

'Diamond Shell' reprinted in the *Prime Year's Best Dark Fantasy and Horror*.

'Six Suicides' winner of the Australian Shadows Award.

She is working in the Zeitgeist of *The Road* and Steven Amsterdam—the apocalypse and afterwards—but at much shorter length. … [T]he stories are succinct and powerful.

The Age

A Book Of Endings, the long-awaited collection of stories by Deborah Biancotti, one of Australia's best writers of short weird fiction (and I do mean weird) from Twelfth Planet Press, is a very tight and beautifully presented book.

Not if You Were the Last Short Story on Earth

Deborah Biancotti's superb collection of short stories reminds me of the engaging work of Robert Aickman. She is a damned fine storyteller and her sheer originality, zest, energy and style fill the dark skyline of the modern world with luminous flares of mysterious force.

Graham Joyce

Many of these are magic realist and surreal tales where Biancotti can meditate on loss and escape. Indeed, as the title *A Book of Endings* suggests, there is a strong apocalyptic theme to the book, though some of these terminations are personal rather than social … There is humour here too though the pervading atmosphere is one of melancholy, which hovers over the pieces … Here we get a glimpse of Biancotti's wonderful prose, which manages to be both evocative and controlled.

Overland

Deborah Biancotti's first collection of short stories is jaw-droppingly good … these stories do what Biancotti's work does best: plumbs the dark everyday. She has a particular talent for reminding the reader that under every ordinary surface there lurks a range of dark rips and tides waiting to pull the unwary beneath … Biancotti's stories are often strange, sometimes frightening and frequently masterful.

ASif!

There's wonder to the world, and a dark magic. And Deborah Biancotti wants to show it to you. Not just a series of short stories but an encyclopaedia of the uncanny, and a haunting reflection of how close the everyday is to madness. This is astonishing stuff – clever, humane, and more than a little profound.

Robert Shearman

Biancotti draws her main characters with deft strokes … I look forward to seeing what this author comes up with next.

SFcrowsnest

Twelve Planets

What are the Twelve Planets?

The Twelve Planets are twelve boutique collections by some of Australia's finest short story writers. Varied across genre and style, each collection will offer four short stories and a unique glimpse into worlds fashioned by some of our favourite storytellers. Each author has taken the brief of 4 stories and up to 40 000 words in their own direction. Some are quartet suites of linked stories. Others are tasters of the range and style of the writer. Each release will bring something unexpected to our subscriber's mailboxes.

When are the Twelve Planets?

The Twelve Planets will spread over 2011 and 2012, with six books released between February and November each year.

The first three titles are *Nightsiders* by Sue Isle (March), *Love and Romanpunk* by Tansy Rayner Roberts (May) and *Thief of Lives* by Lucy Sussex (July).

How to receive the Twelve Planets

The Twelve Planets will be available for purchase in several ways:

Single collections will be priced at $20/$23 International each including postage.

A season's pass will offer the three collections of the season for $50/$65 International including postage and each sent out on release, or on purchase of season's pass.

Full subscriptions to the series are $180/$215 International including postage and each sent out on release.

www.twelfthplanetpress.com

A Book of Endings
by Deborah Biancotti

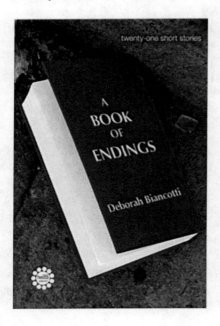

The debut collection from multi-award
winning writer Deborah Biancotti,
including six new works.

www.twelfthplanetpress.com

Horn *Peter M. Ball*

There's a dead girl in a dumpster and a unicorn on the loose. No-one knows how bad that combination can get better than Miriam Aster. What starts as a consulting job for city homicide quickly becomes a tangled knot of unexpected questions, and working out the link between the dead girl and the unicorn will draw Aster back into the world of the exiled fey she thought she'd left behind ten years ago.

Dead girls and unicorns? How warped can this get?

Locus Recommended Reading List

Shortlisted for Best Fantasy Novel and Best Horror Novel, Aurealis Awards

Bleed *Peter M. Ball*

For ten years ex-cop Miriam Aster has been living with her one big mistake—agreeing to kill three men for the exiled Queen of Faerie. But when an old case comes back to haunt her it brings a spectre of the past with it, forcing Aster to ally herself with a stuntwoman and a magic cat in order to rescue a kidnapped TV star from the land of Faerie and stop the half-breed sorcerer who needs Aster's blood.

Shortlisted for Australian Shadow Award for Best Long Work

Glitter Rose

Marianne de Pierres

The *Glitter Rose* Collection features five short stories by
Marianne de Pierres—four previously published and one new
story. Each copy of this limited edition print run is signed and
presented in a beautiful hardbound cover, with internal black
and white illustrations.

The *Glitter Rose* stories are set against the background of Carmine Island (an island reminiscent of Stradbroke Island, Queens-
land) where a decade ago spores from deep in the ocean blew
in, by a freak of nature, and settled on the island. These spores
bring fierce allergies to the inhabitants of the island. And maybe
other, more sinister effects. As we follow Tinashi's journey of
moving to and settling into island life, we get a clearer picture of
just what is happening on Carmine Island.

Sprawl

Sprawl is an exciting new original anthology, glimpsing into the strange, dark, and often wondrous magics that fill the days and nights of Australia's endlessly stretching suburbs.

Liz Argall/Matt Huynh—Seed Dreams (comic)
Peter Ball—One Saturday Night, With Angel
Deborah Biancotti—Never Going Home
Simon Brown—Sweep
Stephanie Campisi—How to Select a Durian at Footscray Market
Thoraiya Dyer—Yowie
Dirk Flinthart—Walker
Paul Haines—Her Gallant Needs
L L Hannett—Weightless
Pete Kempshall—Signature Walk
Ben Peek—White Crocodile Jazz
Tansy Rayner Roberts—Relentless Adaptations
Barbara Robson—Neighbourhood Watch
Angela Slatter—Brisneyland by Night
Cat Sparks—All The Love in the World
Anna Tambour—Gnawer of the Moon Seeks Summit of Paradise
Kaaron Warren—Loss
Sean Williams—Parched (poem)

Locus Recommended Reading List

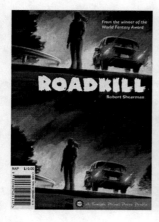

Roadkill *Robert Shearman*

Siren Beat *Tansy Rayner Roberts*

A Twelfth Planet Press Double

Two novelettes—*Roadkill* by Robert Shearman and *Siren Beat* by Tansy Rayner Roberts—published in tête-bêche format form the first Twelfth Planet Press Double.

Roadkill is a squeamishly uncomfortable story with the kind of illicit weekend away that you never want to have.

Siren Beat is a paranormal romance sans vampires or werewolves but featuring a very sexy sea pony. A minor group of man-eating sirens on the docks of Hobart would not normally pose much of a challenge for Nancy, but she is distracted by the reappearance of Nick Cadmus, the man she blames for her sister's death.

Siren Beat
Winner of the WSFA Small Press Short Story Award
Roadkill
Shortlisted for British Fantasy Award for Best Novella